Frank and Joe stole quietly toward the dock. They had followed Vernon, the reporter, hoping to catch him with his source. The Hardys froze as another man walked into the wan glow of a streetlamp. Mark DeCampo, the police commissioner!

"So *he's* the one behind all this!" Joe whispered as Vernon and DeCampo met on the dock. Vernon glanced at his watch. DeCampo peered into the darkness at the edge of the dock.

"Looks like they're waiting for somebody else," Frank said. He watched as Vernon headed back to his car, followed by DeCampo.

"Maybe we should step right up and ask who they're waiting for." Joe put one foot on the dock, but that was as far as he got.

Vernon's car burst into flames with a roar, a tongue of fire licking up from the trunk. Joe and Frank staggered back. The two men closer to the blast were flung headlong, trapped beside the blaze!

Books in THE HARDY BOYS CASEFILES® Series

Available from ARCHWAY Paperbacks

BEYOND THE LAW

Chapter

1

"YOU HAFF ZE DOCUMENTS?" Joe Hardy's blue eyes twinkled as he gave his older brother a lop-sided grin. With an expert twist of the steering wheel, he parked their van in front of Bayport's police headquarters.

"I've got the documents." Frank Hardy held up a thick manila envelope, shaking his head at Joe's hokey accent. "You sound like something out of a bad late-night move." He opened the van door and stepped out into the warm day.

The police headquarters at the top of the stairway before him was a squat, solid-looking building. Its thick, redbrick walls looked as if they'd stood in the middle of Bayport forever. Frank remembered that when he and Joe were kids, they'd joked that headquarters must have been

1

the first thing built in town and that Chief Collig had gotten his start fighting Indians with his boys in blue.

Over the years Frank and Joe had been at headquarters many times, running errands for their father. Fenton Hardy was a private detective, and his investigations often involved his working closely with the police. Frank and Joe tangled with criminals, too, but they usually found themselves competing with the law.

Frank smiled. Chief Collig and the rest of Bayport's Finest found it hard to accept the idea of teenagers solving crimes. But that hadn't stopped him and Joe from putting a lot of crooks behind bars.

"Let's give these papers to the chief," Joe said as they headed up the front steps. "He has to sign off on them before Dad's license can get renewed." Another grin swept his broad, good-humored face. "A simple enough job."

An answering smile appeared on Frank's dark, handsome features. "At least it's dry work. Anything to stay above water." Frank was talking about their last adventure, *Deep Trouble*, in which they'd faced claim jumping and murder while diving for sunken treasure.

Frank pushed the heavy door open and stepped into the cool lobby of the building, grateful to be out of the late summer heat. Frank could hardly believe school would be starting in a little more than a week.

Frank looked around and decided that this place must have been something to see—about fifty years earlier. Now, though, the decoration seemed old-fashioned. The tall inquiries desk just ahead of him looked ready for another fifty years' work, though, even if it was dented and scarred.

Behind the desk and peering down at them was Patrolman Con Riley. A wry smile appeared on his square, ruddy face. "Well, what can we professionals do for Bayport's youngest crime-busters?" he asked. Con was the closest thing to a friend they had on the force, but he was still a cop. Frank couldn't expect a welcome with open arms.

"Can we see Chief Collig, Con?" Frank asked. "Dad sent us with some papers that have to be signed for his P.I. license. So if we can just get them in and out—"

Con shook his head. "I don't think that's a good idea. The chief's in a meeting with the new police commissioner, Mark DeCampo." He frowned. "That guy has really been getting the chief's goat. I guess the chief just hasn't been himself since his wife passed away."

Frank nodded. He and Joe had gone with their parents to the funeral services and been surprised at the turnout. They'd learned that Beatrice Collig had done a lot of good for the community. Although the new wing on the library carried the name of a rich contributor,

Bea Collig was the one who'd led the fund-raising drive. She had organized work-study programs to keep kids in school. And thanks to another plan she had championed, many of the younger police officers were taking college courses.

"Mrs. C. was like a mom to all of us on the force," Riley said sadly. "We miss her, but it's hardest on the chief. His temper has been terrible ever since she, uh, went."

"His temper?" Joe said in disbelief. "Don't take this the wrong way, Con, but how could you tell? Chief Collig is always blowing up at something."

Frank nodded. The chief was well-known for his short fuse, and the Hardys had lit it often by interfering in what Collig considered police business.

"Oh, sure, he gets *red* angry a lot," Con agreed. "His face turns red, he yells a bit, then he calms down. That's normal. No, I'm talking about how he gets *white* angry. All the blood leaves his face, his voice gets quiet, and he talks all polite-like. But when he's done, you feel about this tall." Con held up his hand, his thumb and forefinger about an inch apart.

"What's bugging him so much?" Frank wanted to know.

"Oh, it's the new city government. At first I was glad to see honest people in office. I

believed in the idea of cleaning things up after
that last bunch was kicked out and convicted."

From the look on his face, Con had changed
his mind, Frank decided. "But there's a problem
with this purer than pure image. All the new
bigwigs want to be seen on TV, uncovering corruption. You know how they've reorganized the
Sanitation Department and the mess they found
in the school lunch program. Now DeCampo
wants to find some corruption on the force. So
he went and brought in his own—"

All of a sudden Con's face changed, he sat
straighter in his chair, and his voice became very
crisp. "No, I'm sorry, the chief isn't available
right now," he said to the boys. "You'll have
to— Oh, hello, Captain Lawrence."

"People to see the chief, Riley?" A man in
a carefully tailored police captain's uniform
appeared beside the desk, almost soundlessly.
Frank stared. The guy looked almost like Holly-
wood's version of police brass. Under a cap
whose visor was covered with gold braid, the
man's graying hair had been cut to look profes-
sional but stylish. His teeth, gleaming in a quick
smile, were so white that Frank suspected they'd
been capped. The face above the insignia of rank
was a little too thin to be handsome but probably
looked great on TV.

"Perhaps I can help," the man offered.

"Uh, I don't think so, Captain Lawrence,"

Con said, his voice tight. "The chief will have to sign off on these papers. They're the local approval for Fenton Hardy's private investigator's license. This is Frank and Joe—"

"Hardy?" Captain Lawrence's face suddenly grew cold. "I'm not fond of private eyes, not even the famous Fenton Hardy. And I've heard about you two—the so-called Hardy boys. Kid vigilantes have no business in modern crime control."

Lawrence stepped abruptly away. "I'll be in my office, studying reports," he told Con over his shoulder.

Riley sat stiffly at attention until the man was gone. Then he leaned over the desk, speaking softly. "That's the clown DeCampo has sicced on us," he said in disgust. "Captain Parker Lawrence. Get a load of him—'crime control.' Whatever happened to enforcing the law? He'd rather give the streets to the creeps while he makes cops miserable with investigations by his Internal Affairs Unit."

"Internal Affairs?" Joe repeated. "Aren't those the guys who go probing for crooked cops?"

"That's right. DeCampo's convinced that if the politicians in town were crooked, then the cops have to be, too. So he imported Captain Lawrence to spy on us. And Lawrence tried to get *me* to work as a snitch for him."

"What did you say?" Frank asked.

"I said no, and then I told the chief. He called DeCampo, and that's why they're in there." Con pointed down the hallway behind him to a pebbled-glass door with the word *Chief* in gold letters.

As they watched, two shadows appeared close to the glass, and voices were raised, so Frank and Joe could hear.

"Yeah, Mr. Commissioner. I suspected it was *your* efforts." Chief Collig's voice was as sharp as a knife.

"I mean the *administration's* efforts to clean up the force," Mark DeCampo quickly amended.

"No, I think you were right the first time," Collig returned angrily. "It's *your* efforts to get on TV, like all the other administration crimebusters. Well, let me tell you one thing, pal. You're trying to uncover something that's not there. And your grandstanding is hindering this police force. How do you expect cops on the beat to do their jobs if they always have to look over their shoulders? And why? Because a bunch of clowns are trying to find corruption that doesn't exist. If people don't trust my officers, they can't do their jobs."

"It's not a question of trust, Collig, but of control."

"Now you're saying I can't control my own people? Or is it that *you* want to control them?"

DeCampo's voice turned nasty. "Don't push me, Collig. You're the last major official left from the previous administration, the only one who's not in jail. I could get lots of support to make it a clean sweep," he said threateningly.

"Those crooks didn't appoint me!" Collig's voice was an angry roar.

"Yes, but you worked with them." DeCampo raised his voice to drown out Collig's. "And if you work in the mud, you're bound to get dirty. Hey! What—?"

Frank and Joe stared, amazed, as the two shadows started scuffling.

"I don't believe this," Joe began. His words were cut off as the door to the chief's office suddenly flew open. For a second Mark DeCampo stood facing the hall, framed in the doorway. Frank had seen the police commissioner on TV, but never like this. The man's expensive suit was rumpled, his tie askew, and his handsome face mottled purple with anger. He stumbled a couple of steps down the hall, from the force of being thrown out of the office. "You're finished, Collig," DeCampo choked out, turning back to the office. "You pushed it too hard this time."

Chief Collig gripped the doorframe, breathing hard, his big, stocky frame rigid. Frank noticed that the sleeves on Collig's uniform shirt were rolled up, the muscles on his arms rippling as he tried to calm down.

"Pushed it, DeCampo?" Collig glared at the police commissioner, his face pale. "You're lucky I didn't punch your smug face in for that crack."

Collig raised a clenched fist. "Nobody says that Ezra Collig isn't honest. *Nobody!*"

Chapter

2

FOR A LONG MOMENT the two men stood and glared at each other. Both Joe and Frank leaned against the front desk, trying to appear as inconspicuous as possible. Joe noticed that Con Riley had his head down, too. None of them wanted to be noticed by the two angry men.

Joe didn't even turn as Mark DeCampo stormed down the hall and out the front doors of the building. From the other end of the hall, the door to Chief Collig's office closed with a thunderous slam. The Hardys lifted their heads and raised their eyes toward the closed door. Joe wondered if this was how survivors of heavy shelling felt as they poked their heads up to see where the artillery had been fired from.

Con Riley cleared his throat. "Well, the meeting's over. If you want to go in now, I guess you can.''

"No way, Con." Frank shook his head. "Mount Collig might erupt all over again. Especially if he knew we witnessed his last outburst." He passed the packet of papers to Riley. "Why don't you wait until the chief has calmed down a bit, then give him these to sign. We'll pick them up later—maybe tomorrow."

Con gave them a wicked grin. "Well, if you're sure . . .''

The Hardys hurried out of headquarters like witnesses who didn't want to be tapped for questioning. Joe was sure that when the chief cooled off, he'd be very embarrassed about blowing up. After all, he'd physically thrown Mark DeCampo out of his office. He certainly wouldn't feel better if he discovered he'd had an audience.

When they'd climbed back in the van, Joe finally broke the silence. "Do you believe what happened?" he asked as he started the engine. "That was some show the chief put on. I've seen him mad before, but he never lost it like that."

"Not only that, it's *who* he lost it with," Frank said, frowning. "Strictly speaking, Mark DeCampo is Collig's boss. He could fire the chief for what happened today."

"But he wouldn't," Joe predicted confidently. "He'd have to give a reason, and somehow I don't see him complaining in public that Collig bounced him out of his office.'' He grinned. "DeCampo may want to get on television, but he doesn't want to look stupid.''

"It's not as straightforward as that.'' Frank shook his head. "DeCampo is a politician. He knows there's more than one way to skin a cat.''

Joe glanced over. "What do you mean?''

"I mean DeCampo won't fire Collig right now. But he'll be looking for a reason—any reason—to give the chief his walking papers.''

"Fat chance of that,'' Joe scoffed. "Collig has been running that force for years, and he does a great job. Just a couple of months ago he got that award for being one of the best cops in the country. How can DeCampo touch him?''

"All he needs is one little incident to make Collig look bad,'' Frank said. "The rest of city hall will line up behind him to get rid of the chief.''

Joe was a little shaken. "But that—that sounds crooked. I thought this new bunch was supposed to be honest.''

Frank shrugged. "It's still politics. And the new bunch is a lot more honest than the old one. Remember what happened when *they* had a political problem.''

Joe remembered only too well. Maybe this city government set up committees and dumped on Collig, but the old guard played rough. They even murdered the city manager when they thought he was about to reveal some of their dirty deals. By sheer bad luck the hired killer bumped into Callie Shaw, Frank's girlfriend, while making his getaway. That had put Callie, Frank, and Joe on the hit list, and they'd come frighteningly close to getting killed.

Of course, they'd finally cracked the *See No Evil* case, and by catching the hired killer, they'd launched the scandal that brought the old city government down. In a way, the Hardys had helped to usher in the new government—including Mark DeCampo.

"It's almost funny," Frank said. "Every time we ran up against Collig in a case, Collig got furious with us. Now he's being accused of that same kind of corruption we uncovered in the government."

"So *you* think," Joe said. "The chief's got nothing to worry about."

"What about those threats DeCampo made?" Frank asked.

"You mean that 'clean sweep' crack? What's he going to do? He has no proof that Collig's corrupt."

"DeCampo just has to make Collig look bad," Frank said. "He just needs to make people doubt Collig."

"Collig's got a great reputation," Joe responded. "Who'd doubt—"

"You did, during the *See No Evil* case. That's

why we didn't bring the cops in until the very end.''

"Yeah, but—" Joe decided to shut up. They drove the rest of the way home in silence.

Fenton Hardy was not happy to hear that his papers were still at police headquarters. He was even less happy when he heard why.

"DeCampo told Chief Collig he was finished? He threatened to fire him?" He shook his head in disbelief. "What for?"

The boys explained about the new Internal Affairs Unit and DeCampo's accusations of corruption.

Fenton Hardy surprised his sons by throwing his head back and laughing. "The Bayport force? Corrupt? No way. I was a cop myself in New York. I've known a lot of cops—honest ones and not so honest. Seen all the setups and scams. I've even helped break some up."

His expression grew more serious. "I'd know if anything crooked were going on here. So would Ezra Collig. He's an honest cop if ever I saw one. And I've never seen anyone so down on crooked cops."

"So you think he'll be around tomorrow when we go to pick up your papers?" Joe gave Frank a smug smile as he spoke.

"I certainly hope so," Fenton said. "Of course, with politics and politicians, you can never be sure."

Now it was Frank's turn to act smug as the smile disappeared from Joe's face.

Joe spent the afternoon working on the van. He had a suspicion that the engine's timing was a little off. He usually felt better working with his hands when things were disturbing him.

They couldn't really be thinking of getting rid of Chief Collig. It would be like removing a local landmark.

Joe tried to imagine what the police force would be like without the chief. For all his life—or at least, all the time he'd been investigating crimes—Collig had been there. Usually the chief had acted more like the enemy, an obstacle to solving a mystery. He definitely didn't like competition. He'd get furious when the Hardys contradicted him on a case, and often he'd gnash his teeth when the Hardys turned out to be right.

But the chief also knew good work when he saw it, even when it drove him crazy. For Joe, Collig represented the local law—tough, hardworking, and, Joe was sure, totally honest.

As he bent over the engine with his testing gear, he hesitated for a second. What a shock it would be if the chief lost his job so soon after losing his wife.

Joe set to work, and after a while the questions receded to the back of his mind. There was a job to be done here. Hands and tools moved carefully, tuning the engine.

At last he had the van's engine purring perfectly. "Yeah!" he said, listening to the solid sound. "It runs like a big jungle cat."

"Hey, Joe!" Frank stood in the doorway between the house and the garage. "Come in here. You have to hear this!"

"I've got—" Joe began.

"Forget about the tools! This won't wait!"

Puzzled, Joe followed his brother into the house, wiping his dirty hands on an old rag.

The television was on in the den, the last minutes of an ad for WBPT's "Evening News Hour." The face on the screen was so clean-cut, a choirboy would look sleazy beside it. A deep, serious voice was saying, "Our new newsman, Rod Vernon, brings the hard-hitting style that made him a network news star to Bayport—"

"You can say that again," Frank said grimly.

The pounding newsroom music on the ad faded, only to return again as the show resumed. Joe glanced at his watch. The Bayport "Evening News Hour" had begun.

The camera zoomed in for a tight close-up on Rod Vernon, showing off blue eyes, neatly combed blond hair, and a jaw just rugged enough. His perfect features were set in a very serious expression as he stared out at his audience.

"Tonight's lead story will be a shock to most area residents. We've discovered that a major figure in Bayport's crime-control establishment may be a criminal himself.''

Joe stared as Vernon's face was replaced on the screen by a stock-film clip of Chief Collig in his dress uniform. ''Information received by us indicates that Chief Ezra Collig of the Bayport police force was fired from his first law-enforcement job.''

The picture of Collig's face froze on the screen as Joe stared. ''Apparently,'' Vernon went on, ''Collig had been taking bribes from local businesspeople.''

Chapter

3

FRANK AND JOE STOOD in stunned silence while they listened to the whole lead story. Only when the anchorman's face appeared on the screen, talking about the latest state budget crisis, did they move.

"This is getting weirder and weirder," Joe said. "What do you think of what that Vernon guy was saying?"

Frank abruptly turned off the TV. "I'm more interested in what he *wasn't* saying," he finally replied.

"What do you mean?"

"All of Vernon's 'story' was a rehash of his intro line," Frank explained. "He had nothing new to add after the second sentence."

Joe frowned. "He gave the name of the town where Collig worked—Millerton."

"And the fact that thirty-five years ago Ezra Collig joined the police force there. Then, six months later, he quit. Fine—that's in the public record. But this stuff about collecting bribes . . . there's no record of that—only Vernon saying it, very seriously. If you ask me, he's slicing the bologna mighty fine. I bet he rushed his big exposé onto the air without checking it out."

"So maybe Vernon's wrong," Joe said, a glint of hope in his blue eyes.

Frank shrugged. "Maybe. We can only wait and see."

By the next morning, though, all of Bayport was buzzing with the story. The Hardys were amazed to discover how many people were willing to believe Rod Vernon's accusations. Even the *Bayport Times* had come out with a special edition about the corruption allegations. The front page showed a photo of an incredibly young-looking Ezra Collig. He stood uncomfortably at attention in an ill-fitting police uniform, his eyes focused to the right.

"Looks like he's staring right at the headline," Joe said, holding up the paper while his brother paid for it. Indeed, Collig seemed to be reading the big black letters beside him: "Holding the Bag?"

The boys were standing at the entrance to the

Bayport Mall. Frank had made plans to have lunch with his girlfriend, Callie Shaw, and then to head over to police headquarters to pick up Fenton Hardy's papers.

Inside, the food court was full of people. Frank had to keep Joe from crashing into people as he read the story. Joe finished and folded the paper. "Nothing new in here. It basically reports that Vernon accused Collig on the air of being a bagman—collecting bribes. All that's new is this picture. The caption says it dates from Collig's days on the Millerton force. Oh, and it tells where Millerton is."

"I looked it up on a map last night," Frank said.

"Well, for people like me, who didn't," Joe said, "they give a little map. Hmm. I'd say he moved about as far from that town as he could and still stay in the same state. Funny."

"Oh, hilarious." Frank glanced at the story. "Did the *Times* try getting in touch with the Millerton police?"

Joe held out the paper. "Yeah. According to their records, Collig worked for about six months, then resigned on very short notice. So Collig wasn't fired, the way Vernon said."

"But he did leave," Frank said, frowning. "Which will start everyone wondering if there's a cover-up. They'll figure Collig left Millerton under a cloud." He sighed. "I just hope that cloud doesn't rain on the chief's parade."

Frank forced his way into the lunchtime crowd filling Mr. Pizza. Callie had managed to grab a table; she waved to the boys, who quickly joined her.

"What's up?" Frank noticed that his girlfriend's pretty face had a little more color than usual.

Callie shook her head, her blond hair flying around her shoulders. "It's the radio. They're playing—well, just listen."

The rock song blaring from the pizza joint's speakers came to an end, and the disk jockey came on. "And now we've got a request from yet another of Police Chief Collig's many admirers. Good choice—it may be where the chief ends up. So let's give it up for the King—"

A moment later Elvis Presley began singing "Jailhouse Rock."

"The station's been doing that ever since I came in," Callie said, "which is a pretty lousy thing to do to the chief, if you ask me."

Frank got up and went to the counter to order a pie and sodas, then called the manager over. "Hey, Tony."

Tony Prito was an old pal of Frank and Joe. He dropped the wad of pizza dough he'd been working on into some flour and came over. "How's it going?"

"Not bad. Think you can get another station on the radio, though? Callie's getting a little annoyed at the Collig trash-a-thon."

"Yeah? Well, *we* like it," one of the kids at the counter said loudly. Pizza grease gleamed on his chin. "This is my favorite station, and Howie Starr is my favorite deejay."

"That's right!" other voices said.

Bolstered by the show of support, the greasy-chinned spokesman faced off against Frank. "Maybe you're not as hot a detective as you think, Hardy. After all, you've been sucking up to the police for years, and you never figured that Collig was a crook."

"Yeah!" more voices called.

Frank managed to hold back his anger and keep his voice even. "From everything I've heard so far, there's no proof the chief is a crook."

"The news guy on TV wouldn't have called him one if it wasn't true!" somebody yelled.

"That shows what you know!" Joe Hardy jumped up from his seat. "I have a buddy over at WBPT, a cameraman we used to work with. He shoots the in-studio stuff for the 'Evening News Hour.' You've seen all those ads about what a hotshot network news reporter Rod Vernon is? Ever wonder why he's doing local news in Bayport? He's a troublemaker and got sent down to the minor leagues. The guy likes to come up with big scandals, but about a third of the time he practically invents them."

Frank was a little surprised at his brother's statement. He'd noticed Joe spending time on the phone that morning but hadn't dreamed that he was checking up on Rod Vernon.

The kid with the greasy chin stood silent for a second. Then his face brightened as he came up with a comeback. "Yeah, well, that means the guy is *right* about two-thirds of the time, and I think he's got the chief pegged."

More voices joined in, egging Greasy-chin on.

"What do you guys know?" Callie shouted angrily. "You've never even met Chief Collig!"

"We saw him at school for anticrime assemblies," one kid said. "I never liked him."

The song on the radio had changed to another "humorous" request—Johnny Cash's "Folsom Prison Blues." Then the hourly news came on.

"Still no comment from Chief Ezra Collig on the bribery accusations made by Bayport newscaster Rod Vernon—"

"See?" The kid at the counter finally wiped his greasy chin. "If he's innocent, why doesn't he come out and say so?"

The voice of the radio announcer continued as Frank and Joe walked back to join Callie. "We've made repeated inquiries at Bayport Police Headquarters, but the only response we've had came from Captain Parker Lawrence of the Internal Affairs Unit."

Joe shot Frank a worried look. Why was Internal Affairs involved?

Then came Lawrence's voice. "Police Commissioner DeCampo has asked for a thorough and fair investigation. I shall be appointing my best people—"

"For a political hatchet job," Frank said in disgust. "DeCampo has his incident to get rid of Collig now, and he can have the guy he hired do the job. All he has to do is drag his feet on this so-called investigation and let the media hang Collig out to dry."

"But we know the chief would never do the things they're saying," Callie objected.

"Just look at them." Frank jerked his head at the hooting crowd in the pizza joint.

"Kind of scary," Joe said quietly. "Like that moron saying, 'I heard it on TV, so it must be right.' "

Frank stared at the newspaper, taking in the picture of the young Ezra Collig. He couldn't have been much older than I am, Frank thought. The face was much thinner, but those were definitely Collig's features.

Frank's eyes narrowed with a sudden thought. "I wonder where the *Bayport Times* got this picture. It sure was convenient."

"Maybe they were working on the story already," Callie suggested.

"Uh-uh," Frank said. "What they've got here in print is only what Vernon said on TV, plus what they could pick up in a quick phone call to the Millerton police."

He turned to Callie. "Do you think your

friend Liz Webling is working at the *Times* today?''

"Why don't we go and find out?" Callie said.

"After we eat," Joe added.

There was almost half a pizza on the table when they did leave. None of them had much of an appetite, after all.

After a quick drive downtown Callie, Frank, and Joe found Liz Webling at the *Times* offices, pounding a typewriter and frowning. She seemed happy to leave her job and talk for a few minutes. "Dad always sticks me with the boring stuff, like typing up the notes from the school board meeting," she complained.

"Want to try something a little hotter?" Callie said. "How about the Collig story?"

Liz's dark eyes sharpened. "What have you got on that?" she asked. "All we have is Rod Vernon's word, plus a call we made to the Millerton police."

"And an old photo of Collig," Frank pointed out. "Was that an old file thing?"

Liz shook her head. "No. We got it last night." She went to a nearby desk and pulled out a file folder. Inside was an old black-and-white photo—the picture of the young Ezra Collig. A box had been drawn on the picture in grease pencil. "That's where we cropped the shot," Liz explained. "We didn't want to use the whole picture."

"Hey, it's only half a picture," Joe said, fin-

gering the right-hand side. There was no bor-
der—whatever had been there was snipped away
clean.

"That's the way we got it," Liz said. "I
remember wondering what Collig was looking
at."

"What do you mean, you got it last night?"
Frank asked.

"A messenger delivered it just a bit after the
newscast," Liz replied.

"Something for you to make up a front page
around," Frank said suddenly. "Somebody is
really pressing all the media buttons around
here. We're definitely looking at a setup."

"Setup? Who?" Liz scooped up her notepad.
"Are you guys investigating? Do you have any
suspects in mind?"

"No comment," Frank said hurriedly.

Liz grimaced in disappointment. "Give me a
break here, guys," she said. "Here I am, mind-
ing the store while everybody goes to the big
press conference at the cop house. And you
hand me a story—"

"Press conference? At police headquarters?"
Frank broke in.

"Yeah." Liz blinked in confusion as her three
visitors whipped around and headed for the
door.

"How are we going to get in?" Joe wanted to
know.

26

"We play it dumb—we're just three kids coming in to pick up Dad's papers."

As he led the way to police headquarters, Frank found the street in front of the building full of news vans. "Looks like a riot," he whispered to Joe and Callie as they slipped through the entrance. The lobby was jammed. Camera crews elbowed one another, jockeying for position in front of the booking desk. Behind them were the still photographers. A late reporter jostled Frank as he ran past him to join the crowd. The guy acted like the last wolf to get to the deer.

Confronting the whole media mob was a lone police officer—Con Riley. He looked as if he wished he were anywhere else, Frank thought. "Will you folks please stop shoving?" he shouted over the noise. "I've already told you, Chief Collig isn't in."

"Then who's holding the press conference?" Frank recognized Rod Vernon in the middle of the crowd. His blond hair was immaculately moussed and brushed into a shining helmet, and his WBPT news blazer was perfectly cut and unwrinkled, but there was a nasty expression on his choirboy face. "I don't like dealing with underlings—"

Behind Con, down the hall, the door to the chief's office opened and Mark DeCampo stepped out. Frank wondered how anyone could believe the smile on the man's tanned face. Marching

27

behind DeCampo was Parker Lawrence, the life-size toy soldier.

"I'd like to thank our friends in the media for taking the time to attend this briefing," DeCampo said. His "media friends" were all busily aiming minicams, cameras, microphones, and cassette recorders at him.

"I'll keep my comments brief," DeCampo said. "In response to the questions being raised about Ezra Collig, I have suspended him from the office of chief of police, pending a full investigation."

Frank did a slow burn, watching DeCampo turn to his Internal Affairs stooge. "In the meantime, Captain Parker Lawrence will run the investigation—as well as the Bayport police force."

Chapter

4

FRANK WAS TOO STUNNED to move, but the media hounds around him sprang into action. Hands shot up, and questions were shouted. "Mr. Commissioner!" they chorused. "Does this mean you believe the charges of bribery?"

Mark DeCampo was too polished a politician to fall for that. He ignored the questions, instead turning the conference over to Captain Parker Lawrence. Frank had to admit that Lawrence was quite a performer. For the next forty-five minutes he showed himself to be honest, true, forthright—all the best Boy Scout virtues. At the same time, however, Lawrence did his best to stick a knife in Chief Collig's back.

Inwardly Frank seethed, but he knew that all

he could do for now was listen to Lawrence's rhetoric.

Lawrence never mentioned Collig's guilt or innocence. He just made nice noises about bringing the investigation to a speedy conclusion.

When the newspeople began asking how long the investigation would take, however, Lawrence gave them a lot of double-talk. And he asked to be addressed as Acting Chief Lawrence.

When the reporters realized they weren't going to get anything more, they disappeared with surprising speed. So did Lawrence, once no more cameras were around.

The Hardys and Callie found themselves alone in the big, old-fashioned lobby, except for Con Riley behind the booking desk.

"So what did you think?" Con asked quietly. He threw a glance over his shoulder toward the chief's office. "I think this guy is gonna slaughter the chief, then hang the pieces out to dry." He wrinkled his nose as if he'd just detected an extremely bad smell. "Acting Chief, my foot. He's the boss now, and he intends to stay in that office. With him running the investigation— and that rat DeCampo taking care of the political side—they'll do it."

"Con, we hate to bother you now, but what about—"

"Your dad's papers!" Con smacked himself in the forehead. "I got them in to the chief yesterday, but I don't think he signed them." He frowned. "And I don't know if it's a good idea for me to check right now."

"Don't worry about it, Con," Frank said. "We'll ask Dad what he wants to do."

"You might have to get them signed by the Acting Chief." Con gave a grim laugh. "Do you think that would make him an acting P.I.?"

Con became deadly serious and almost pleaded. "You guys have to stick your noses into this one. You *have* to!"

Frank opened his mouth, but no words came out. "We'll do what we can," he finally said. Callie and Joe silently followed him out of headquarters. They walked to the van, and Frank drove Callie to her house. Then the Hardys headed home to report the latest to their father.

"I can't get over Con asking us for help," Joe said from the passenger seat.

Frank nodded. "It's almost scary to think Collig might need it." He paused for a second. "But I think he does. There are too many people after his hide—Vernon, Lawrence, DeCampo. Take your pick of whoever started this mess."

"You left out 'all of the above,' " Joe told him as they reached their street. He shook his head. "I think we've got to do something, Frank. I mean, Chief Collig can be a pain in the neck. He drives me crazy half the time, but—"

"Hey, the other half you drive him crazy," Frank cut in.

"But he's not a man who'd take bribes. I can't

believe he's guilty." Joe glanced at his brother, but Frank said nothing.

"Well, do you?" Joe asked.

"I wonder how this story got started," Frank finally said. "And why the chief isn't saying anything in his own defense." He sat a little straighter in the driver's seat. "But I think we definitely should look into this whole mess. Until then, well, let's say I'm keeping an open mind."

"I always thought you had a hole in your head." Joe grinned as they pulled into the driveway.

They found their father in his office, hanging up the phone.

"There's still a holdup over your papers," Frank reported. "Looks like Chief Collig didn't sign them yesterday. And today—well, he wasn't in his office."

"Not surprising, after the witch-hunt that's being stirred up." Fenton Hardy scowled. "As a matter of fact, I was just trying to reach Collig at his home. He has to make some sort of a statement."

"Dad, what's he going to do?" Joe asked.

"Make it clear that he's innocent," Fenton said. "Collig is no crook. I'd stake my reputation on that. But I think he's going to need help proving it."

The boys' father gestured toward the phone. "But Collig's phone has been busy for the last

32

hour. He probably just left the receiver off the hook."

"So what do we do now?" Joe said.

"We'll pay him a visit." Fenton gave them a ghost of a smile. "Besides, maybe we'll be lucky and discover he brought my papers home with him."

He got up from his desk chair. "No time like the present. We'll take my car."

Chief Collig lived at the edge of town. Frank stared out the car window at the stone and plaster houses in the quiet neighborhood. But as they rounded a curve in the road, the peace and quiet abruptly disappeared in a welter of parked cars and a milling crowd.

"Now we know where all those media people went after the press conference," Frank said, recognizing two of the TV vans that had blocked the street in front of headquarters.

Now they were blocking the road in front of Collig's house. Camera crews, photographers, and reporters crowded onto the chief's lawn.

Frank realized there wasn't enough room on the road for Fenton to get through. They came to an abrupt stop and climbed out, leaving the car to block the road even more. Frank found himself staring down dozens of camera lenses.

Rod Vernon was in the lead, his video operator at his side. "Outside the home of embattled Bayport police chief Ezra Collig, we find famous private detective Fenton Hardy."

Why do these news types always have to hang idiotic tags on people? Frank wondered. It's not enough to call Collig the police chief. He's got to be "embattled." Just as Dad has to be a "famous private detective."

Vernon gave them a friendly grin as he shoved a mike into Fenton's face. "Can it be that the police chief feels so desperate that he's turned to outside help?"

Fenton didn't reply.

"So you aren't coming to see Chief Collig?" Vernon pressed.

Frank stared at the guy's face. Those choirboy features were still set in a smile, but the eyes were like those of an animal—an animal that had smelled blood.

"No comment," Fenton Hardy said. "Now, would you please move your van so we can get by?"

"Yeah," Joe added. "Tell your guy to stop wasting film and our time."

As soon as he told the video operator to cut, Vernon stopped wasting his smile on them, too. He didn't bother to hide his annoyance as he sent his sound man to move the WBPT van.

With the road cleared, Fenton and the boys slid back in and drove on.

"How are we going to get in the house with that mob in front of the place?" Joe asked.

"Not through the front door, that's for sure." Frank glanced from the crowd of media people

34

to the road ahead. "The road curves a bit more, winding up into the hills. We could probably park out of sight up there, then cut across on foot to Collig's backyard." He looked over toward his father. "Feel up to a little cross-country trek, Dad?"

Fenton Hardy smiled. "Let's head for the hills."

They drove on, following the road up a hillside. Fenton pulled the car over in front of a small yellow bungalow. Below them they could see a thin row of trees, separating the yard behind the yellow house from the Collig backyard.

"No fence—that's a piece of luck," Joe said.

"And there don't seem to be any newspeople hanging around the back," Frank added.

His father stared at the grassy slope. "They haven't mowed this part of the lawn recently, but it looks fairly straightforward. Let's hope the folks who live here don't think we're burglars."

They left the car, moving silently past the yellow house. Frank held his breath as they passed dark windows. Then he had to concentrate on keeping his footing. The slope was steeper than it seemed, and he found himself skidding on the long grass until they reached the cover of the scrubby set of trees.

Peering around the bushes and thin tree trunks, they checked out the open space of Chief Collig's backyard.

"Nothing to hide behind at all," Fenton Hardy said. "Let's hope Vernon and his merry crew are all hypnotized by the front door. I don't want them asking us more stupid questions."

Frank took a deep breath, then dashed across the carefully tended back lawn to the rear door of the house.

"I sure hope the chief is home," Joe muttered as they ran. "We'll look real stupid banging on the door of an empty house."

Ten feet from the door, they discovered the house was occupied, all right. The back door flew open.

There stood Chief Collig, a wild look in his eye—and a .38 caliber police revolver in his hand.

Chapter

5

THE HARDYS MOMENTARILY FROZE under Ezra Collig's gun. As recognition came into the chief's eyes, the weapon went down, and a shaky hand came up to rub his forehead.

"I was in the kitchen, keeping away from that pack of vultures parked on my porch," Collig said. "When I saw people in the yard, I decided to come out and . . ." He suddenly became aware of the gun in his hand and stopped speaking. "Uh, I was going to warn them off."

Fenton was serious as he and the boys entered the house. "You should be glad we *weren't* newspeople," Fenton told the chief. "A picture of you waving a gun at them would have been front-page material."

Collig shuddered and put the gun in a drawer.

"I can imagine the headline—'Is Chief Losing His Mind?'" He dropped into a chair and stared out through the mesh curtains on the room's big picture window. The kitchen must have been a more recent addition to the old house. Frank saw an ultramodern range and all sorts of appliances for processing and preparing food.

"You don't know what it's like," Collig said, still staring out through the curtain. "I haven't had a moment's peace since that creep Vernon went on TV last night. First came the call from DeCampo, asking me not to come in today. Then the phone didn't stop ringing. I finally took it off the hook." Frank saw the receiver from the kitchen wall phone stuck in a drawer.

"I couldn't get out of the house, not with that crowd outside." Collig's face was bitter. "And it just kept getting larger."

"It will keep growing until you go out and say something. You're the only one who hasn't been heard from in this story." Fenton gazed at Collig with concern. "You realize, of course, that they're going to keep hounding you."

"Hounding me?" Collig repeated. "You make it sound like they've got a right to treat me like a criminal."

"Look, I don't think there's anything to this story. Neither do the boys or a lot of people in Bayport. That's why we're here, to offer our—"

"Help?" Collig cut him off with one angry word. "I've been living in and working in this town for most of my life. Keeping the streets safe, keeping the people safe. If they can't trust me after all that—well, maybe they deserve a tin soldier like Parker Lawrence.

"You never know which are the best years of your life—until they're over," Collig continued. "Those weren't easy years. People don't realize what police work was like, back when I started out. Hardy, you were a cop—what? Twenty years ago?"

Fenton Hardy nodded. "Just about."

"So you know how things have changed. Me, I was an old-timer twenty years ago, with almost fifteen years on the job. It was like another world. Some of the stuff that was a regular part of the job then would be considered criminal today."

Frank almost said that bribery had always been a crime, even back then, but he forced the words back.

Collig's face was grim. "I put in thirty-five years of honest service. Then someone digs up this piece of ancient history to smear me." His hands clenched. "I'm going to find the guy who's pulling this"—he glanced at Fenton Hardy—"myself. And when I track him down, he'll wish he'd never been born."

There was a long, uncomfortable silence after that speech. Obviously, Frank thought, being held a virtual prisoner in his own house hadn't helped the chief's temper.

Fenton Hardy must have thought so, too. "Well, first you'll have to get out of here—and you can't do that until you talk to the people outside."

Collig led the way to the living room. Heading to the window, he twitched back the drape to peek out. The movement must have caught the attention of the newspeople outside. Through the tiny chink in the curtain, Frank saw Rod Vernon's video operator charge forward. He crashed into a blooming rosebush, trying to peer inside.

Hands clenched, Ezra Collig yanked the drapes shut. "My wife planted that bush and tended it for twenty years." His words were quiet, but they simmered with barely contained fury. "And that blasted snoop tramples it down."

Frank was glad that Collig had put his gun away, especially when the man stormed the door.

The Hardys stepped back, out of the line of sight, as Collig opened the door and stepped onto the porch. "I expect you have all been waiting for me to make a statement," the chief began. "Well, here it is. I have no comment on the whispering campaign that is being directed against me."

"How can you really consider it a whispering campaign when all the major news media in the area are carrying the story?" Rod Vernon was in the first rank of reporters, his microphone thrust in Collig's face.

"No comment."

"It would seem that Commissioner DeCampo is taking the allegations very seriously," Vernon pressed. "Are you aware that you've been suspended?"

Collig gave him a look of pure murder. "No comment."

"Could you explain why you left your first police job?" Vernon tried to step around Collig to get into the house. Suddenly he found himself bouncing back from Collig's outflung arm.

"I came out here to make a statement, not invite you into my house to badger me." Collig's voice was ice-cold. "You guys are always ready to yell 'privacy' when cops try to get background on a guy. And your notes are confidential when we want to look at them. But when you want a story, it's fine to come poking and prying into someone's private life, destroying things." He glanced at the trampled rosebush, and his lips became a tight line. "So let me clue you in on something. This is private property, and I want all of you off it—now!"

"Or what?" Rod Vernon asked nastily. "You'll call the cops?"

For a second Frank wondered if Collig was going to burst into a rage. Even Vernon stepped back. But all Collig said was "No comment!"

He slipped back in through the door and slammed it in Vernon's face.

It may not have been a successful press conference, but it served its purpose. Most of the media people began packing up and heading off. "I expect a few diehards will stay out there," Collig said, still grim. "At least that so-called human being, Vernon, has left."

He glanced at Fenton and the boys. "I suppose you'll want to be going, too. Front door or back?"

"Back," Fenton Hardy promptly responded. "We had a run-in with Vernon and his friends, too."

Collig led them to the kitchen door and opened it. Fenton Hardy hesitated for a moment before stepping out. "Good luck, Ezra," he said. "And if you need—"

"Hardy, I know you mean well." Collig raised his hand, cutting Fenton off. "But thanks, anyway." He nodded to Frank and Joe.

The Hardys climbed the hill to their car and took off for home. Each was wrapped in thoughtful silence. At last Frank said, "So what do you think, Dad?"

Fenton Hardy shook his head. "I still believe he's an honest man—but an honest man with something to hide."

"What?" Joe wondered.

"Who knows? But something about this affair has Collig bothered and running a bit scared."

They arrived home to find the answering machine on Fenton's office phone blinking. While their father dealt with the message, the boys talked in the kitchen.

"Come on, Frank. The chief is a good guy. Whatever he's worried about—well, it may be nothing. Just an old embarrassment."

"Sure. Whenever I feel embarrassed, I grab a gun and threaten to take potshots at anybody in my backyard." Frank frowned as he poured himself a glass of milk. "Whatever it is, it's really got the chief off balance."

Fenton Hardy joined them. "The Pittman case is heating up," he announced. "That means I have to get on a plane to Florida right away. While I'm gone"—he sighed—"I suppose there's nothing I can say to keep you off the Collig case. I do have a job for you, though. Track down my papers and get them signed, will you? The licensing authority will start to get impatient."

Frank and Joe spent the evening relaxing as their mother, Laura, helped their father get ready for at least a week-long stay. The boys' aunt Gertrude was out of town, so Frank and Joe watched the evening news alone. Rod Vernon had edited his "interview" with Collig into a real hatchet job.

"Even without the gun Vernon managed to

make Collig look like a real looney-tune." Joe's forehead was creased with worry.

"Yeah, but he's still not presenting anything to back up what he said yesterday," Frank pointed out. "Let's pay a visit to headquarters tomorrow to see if the cops have found out anything solid."

The next morning Frank and Joe climbed the steps of police headquarters. Con Riley sat behind the booking desk. Apparently, he'd recovered from the media onrush.

"Well, gentlemen," he said when he saw the Hardys. "What can we do for you today?"

"Any news on our dad's papers?" Frank asked as he walked up to the desk.

"I've got good news and bad news about that," Con replied. "The papers have been found, but they're in the clutches of our acting chief."

Frank lowered his voice, glancing around. "And how is the acting chief doing on his investigation of the real chief?" he asked.

Even though no one was around, Riley lowered his voice, too. "It's supposed to be top-secret," he said. "But Lawrence and his troops decided to start off by questioning old members of the Bayport force." He grinned without humor. "And old cops love to gossip."

Riley shook his head. "But that's all Lawrence has—rumor and gossip. The old-timers say Collig was a real straight-arrow. He wouldn't go for any scams that were considered okay back then. As he rose in rank, he cracked down on those, too.''

''I guess Lawrence is disappointed at what he found—or *didn't* find out,'' Frank commented.

''The best Lawrence has been able to come up with is a gap in the records. There are a couple of months between the time Collig left his job in Millerton and joined the force here in Bayport.''

Con pitched his voice so it sounded like that of an announcer doing a commercial for a soap opera. ''What was Collig up to? What was he living on? His ill-gotten gains? What terrible secrets will be discovered? Tune in tomorrow—''

''Riley!''

Con jumped. He and the boys turned to look down the hall at the chief's office. There stood a scowling Parker Lawrence. ''If you're finished entertaining your young visitors, Patrolman, perhaps you can send them back here.'' He turned and stepped back into his office.

Poor Con Riley looked like a balloon with all the air let out. ''I, uh, think the acting chief wants a word with you,'' he said.

The chief's office was pretty much the same: big wooden desk, old-fashioned desk lamp, but already a couple of new items had appeared. A computer sat on a table behind the desk, and a TV and VCR faced Parker Lawrence as he sat in the office chair.

Great, Frank thought. Now he can tape all his adventures.

Another thing struck Frank as being just the same. The acting chief gave them the same unfriendly stare that Ezra Collig had often aimed at them across this desk.

"I caught the tail end of that—performance—outside," Lawrence said. "You're trying to dig up information about my investigation. I want you to know that I know you and your father were at Collig's house yesterday."

He slammed a palm down on the desk—a fine dramatic gesture. Frank wondered if Lawrence had been practicing at home. "Obviously, you're planning to interfere in this case—but I won't have it!"

Joe saw red. "What are you going to do? Throw us in jail?"

Lawrence shook his head. "No, I'm just expressing my concern," he said in a silky voice. "I wouldn't want you to distract me from my job, because if I get too busy, I won't be able to sign these." He held up the manila envelope full of Fenton's papers.

"It would be a shame if your father lost his license because you wouldn't listen to reason."

"The nerve of that guy!" Joe slapped the passenger-side panel of the van. Lawrence is blackmailing us!"

Frank nodded from behind the driver's wheel.

46

"But we learned something. Two somethings, in fact. There's an information pipeline between Lawrence and Vernon. We weren't on TV last night. So how did he know we'd passed Collig's house?"

"Do you think maybe Lawrence is the one behind smearing Collig?" Joe suggested.

"Uh-uh," Frank said. "Lawrence may be exploiting and using it, but he's not the brains behind it."

"How do you figure that?" Joe frowned.

"He's a glory hound. Why do you think he has a VCR in his office? So he can see himself on TV. The only thing he cares about is his image. He's not the kind of guy to dig out a story or evidence—he's just a user. If he had solid evidence to get rid of Collig, he'd have it out by now."

"Right," Joe said. "Then who can have started the smear campaign? Who's the brains behind this? Who else do we have? Vernon? DeCampo? Mr. X from planet Y?"

"Judging from yesterday's newscast, Vernon hasn't got any real evidence against Collig, but he's obviously the media connection. Whoever's behind this fed him the initial rumors and stuff."

"So maybe we should keep an eye on Rod Vernon," Joe said, "because he might lead us to a suspect."

A quick call to their contact at the TV station told them where Rod Vernon's WBPT van was.

They arrived at the scene of a fire just in time to see the van pull away. Frank followed cautiously, right back to the television station.

"Great," Joe said as they pulled up across from the station's parking lot. "Now we're stuck on a stakeout."

After the TV van was parked, Rod Vernon didn't head into the building. He cut across the lot to a bright red Porsche Carrera and jumped into the driver's seat. With a throaty rumble the engine started and Vernon headed out.

"At least it's an easy car to spot," Frank said.

They followed the red car through downtown Bayport to the outskirts of town. Just across the bridge over the Willow River, a figure in a trench coat stepped out from behind a tree and waved. Vernon pulled off the road, and the figure slipped into his car.

"The elusive Mr. X," Joe said. "What now? We can't stop on the bridge to check them out."

"We'll pull past, find a place to hide the van, and make our way back." Frank sped up a little, passing Vernon's car. They couldn't get a good look at anyone in the low-slung sports model.

"Over there," Joe said, pointing. "We can park between those bushes."

Frank pulled the van neatly off the road. Then they got out, and closed the doors silently. "Stick to the brush at the side of the road," Frank said. "Don't let them spot us."

He pushed aside some prickly branches. In a

moment he'd have a clear view of who Vernon was conspiring with.

But he didn't get a chance to see. Instead, Frank heard only the roar of a car engine. A black car was streaking across the bridge, heading straight for Vernon's Porsche.

Vernon gunned his engine, slamming the car into gear, and the red sports car roared away.

Both cars screamed down the road in a high-speed chase!

Chapter

6

"CAUGHT FLATFOOTED," Joe said in disgust as the two cars roared past them.

"Well, come on!" Frank shouted, taking off for the van. Joe beat his brother to the door, flung himself in behind the steering wheel, and flipped the key in the ignition. Frank managed to close his door as the van tore out of the bushes.

"Can we catch them?" Frank asked as Joe goosed the gas pedal.

"The dark car, for sure. That's just a regular sedan." Joe was quietly confident of their van. "As for Vernon's Porsche, well, I guess we'll have to be lucky."

They headed down River Road, moving farther away from town.

"There they are!" Frank said as they rounded a curve.

The two cars raced along, far ahead of them. As they whipped along the curves in the country road, the black car stayed right on the tail of the red one.

"Hmm," Joe said. "That sedan has to be a special model, with a muscle engine."

"What we need is a little more muscle in *this* engine," Frank complained. They'd reached a long straightaway, but despite Joe's best efforts, they were hundreds of yards behind the other two cars.

"Hey, I built this van to move fast, but not to challenge every road rocket that comes along." Joe sounded a little embarrassed. "You can't win them all."

As it turned out, they did win one. They were still well behind when a police cruiser came tearing out of the brush ahead of them, siren wailing.

Joe slowed down. No way was he going to pass a cop car while moving well over the speed limit. As they followed, hanging back well behind the action, they saw the police car had the same problem they had had. Not enough speed.

"Looks like a tough chase for the cops," Joe said.

Finally the flashy sports car increased its lead over its black pursuer. The sedan pulled off to the side, and the police pounced, cutting it off.

Moments later the Hardys passed, going at a very slow speed. A red-faced police officer was writing a ticket for a red-faced driver. Joe and Frank both had plenty of time to recognize the man in the black car.

It was Chief Collig.

Later that day the boys learned that Rod Vernon had recognized his pursuer, too. The highlight of the "Evening News Hour" was a report from police headquarters about Collig's speeding ticket.

Joe shook his head and turned off the television. "The chief really blew it this time."

"He blew it for us, too." Frank flopped back on the couch. "If he'd held off for two seconds more, we'd have seen who was in the car with Vernon."

"Cut him some slack, Frank. How could he know we were there?" Joe protested. "Besides, he came up with the same idea you did—tailing Vernon. With a little luck he might have caught the guy in the car. He just has to get used to working the street again. He's a little rusty from running the police force, instead of being out on the streets, investigating."

For two days the Hardys kept an eye on Rod Vernon. They also grew steadily more worried as they realized just how rusty Ezra Collig's surveillance methods were. They could spot the chief a mile off, and so, unfortunately, could Vernon.

Three times during the first day they saw Collig's black sedan roar into humiliating camera ambushes. At one point Vernon's red sports car had stopped to pick up someone from a bus shelter. Collig continued to pursue aggressively. Suddenly the WBPT van screeched out of a side street, door open with a video operator hanging out. Vernon hopped from his car, a mike in his hand, and began asking Collig why he was harassing them.

That was the piece that appeared on the "Evening News Hour" that night.

The next day Collig became more cautious. He borrowed someone else's car to tail Vernon.

He was still spotted, though. Late in the day Vernon led him on a wild-goose chase, then parked in the lot at the Bayport Mall. Pursuing Vernon on foot, Collig ran into the Food Hall—and found another camera crew lying in wait.

"Why are you following me, Mr. Collig?" Vernon asked tauntingly in front of a large audience. "Why can't you let me do my job in peace? Or are you afraid of what I'll find?"

Teeth clenched, Collig wheeled around and walked away, pursued by the camera crew.

"Acting Chief Parker Lawrence has promised me police protection if you continue to harass me." Vernon's smug smile made Joe's stomach churn.

He and Frank were at the edge of a crowd of gawkers who had gathered. The boys made sure they were out of camera range. They didn't want their father to lose his license just because they turned up on Parker Lawrence's VCR.

Joe heard an odd conversation as the camera crew was packing up.

"You know," a young woman with a baby said to another shopper, "that's not fair. Why is this Vernon guy allowed to take Chief Collig apart, but the chief can't even try to find out what Vernon is up to?"

The friend nodded. "I thought maybe there was a case against Collig when they first announced this bribery thing. But we haven't seen any evidence about it on TV—just this Vernon showing poor Chief Collig up."

Frank had obviously been listening in, too. "Let's stop off at Mr. Pizza," he said suddenly.

"What about Vernon?"

"He'll be back at the studio, editing his latest little video footage. I want to catch some more public opinion."

They stopped at the entrance to the pizza shop. Inside, the kid with the greasy chin was chewing on yet another slice. "That was really some show out there. Vernon made Old Man Collig look like a jerk." The kid gave a loud horselaugh.

But instead of joining in, most of the kids in the shop were quiet.

"It was a pretty lousy trick, setting him up like that," one girl said.

"Come on! He caught Collig in the act!"

"In the act of what?" Callie Shaw whipped around from the counter, where she'd been getting a soda. "Following someone is no crime."

"It's harassment." The loudmouth tried to drum up support.

"What's calling a guy a crook without any proof?" one of his friends suddenly asked.

"The cops are checking into it," the loudmouth said sullenly.

"They haven't found anything, though. Neither have the TV reporters or the newspapers." The Hardys' friend Chet Morton put his slice of pizza down. "It's beginning to seem as if Rod Vernon shot his mouth off without any facts. I think they call that libel."

The kid chewed on that for a second, then said, "Well, Collig is a public figure. Doesn't that make it all right?"

"And what's Vernon—an unknown? Why can't Collig follow him? He isn't trying to shoot him or anything. He just wants to know what Vernon's doing. Why is Vernon getting so bent out of shape?"

"Unless," Callie said, "he hasn't got anything to back up his bluff."

"Hey, Charlie," Tony Prito said to the kid who'd been sounding off. "You finished with that slice? Maybe you'd like to take a walk in the mall.''

Joe and Frank exchanged smiles as they ambled in for their dinner.

After that evening's telecast of the "Evening News Hour," Joe felt that a lot more folks would be on Collig's side. Instead of destroying Collig, Vernon was making people sympathetic to the police chief.

The next morning's *Bayport Times* editorial asked some very pointed questions.

Why was Rod Vernon making accusations he couldn't support? If he'd been told that Collig had collected bribes, why didn't he furnish specific proof? And why didn't the anonymous accuser step forward?

Frank folded the newspaper after they finished reading. "This time around we'll really have to keep an eye on Vernon," he said. "I'm betting that whoever is behind this will have to meet with him now. The smear campaign is losing momentum. They'll have to try something new."

Joe called his camera operator friend at WBPT, Johnny Berridge.

"Vernon is really catching some heat for this Collig thing," Berridge told him. "I think he's getting rattled. I overheard his assistant calling a local rental agency to get a car. Something tells me he may ditch his sharp wheels for something a little less noticeable.''

"Like what?" Joe wanted to know.

Berridge's voice dropped low. "Like a brown sedan, license plate ZWD-one-nine-zero."

"That's a rental plate, all right," Joe said.

"It's parked across the street from the station, not in the lot," his contact went on. "Look, I've got to go. Hope this helps."

All day Vernon drove around in his flashy sports car or rode around in the WBPT van. Frank spotted Chief Collig, back in his black sedan. Vernon must have recognized the car, too, but he didn't try any camera attacks. The two of them, with Frank and Joe bringing up the rear, just drove around all day, an auto version of follow the leader.

At last Vernon arrived back at the station in time for the "Evening News Hour" telecast. Collig pulled into the parking lot, and Frank directed Joe to a spot on the street to continue their surveillance.

"I want to keep an eye on the lot and on that rental car on the street," he said.

They spent a boring hour and a half on the stakeout. Then, Joe exclaimed, "Pay dirt!" Rod Vernon dashed from the front door of the studio and hopped into the rental car.

As the Hardys pulled out to follow, Joe shot a quick glance back into the WBPT parking lot. "Should we just leave the chief sitting there?" he asked.

"He fouled up our chance of seeing who Ver-

non was meeting the last time,'' Frank said.
''Not again.''

This time Vernon headed for Bayport's downtown area.

''He's running out of streets,'' Joe said.
''That's the bay up there.''

Following him, they drove through a dingy
neighborhood. Frank saw stained brick ware-
houses with sagging doors, and an occasional
cheap restaurant, all closed now.

Joe hit the brakes suddenly. ''He's driving out
onto that dock.''

''A good place to meet. They can guarantee
nobody else will come too close.''

Joe turned off his headlights and coasted to a
stop about a block from the dock. ''The corner
up there has a broken streetlight,'' he said, jumping out of the van. ''Maybe we can use the shadows to move in closer.''

He led the way, half-crouching through the
darkness. The street was covered with litter, and
it was hard to move without making any noise.
He and Frank reached a half-rotted shed at the
foot of the dock when they heard somebody
behind them kick over an empty soda can.

The Hardys froze as a man walked out from
a shadowy side street into the wan glow of a
streetlamp. Mark DeCampo!

''So *he's* the one behind all this,'' Joe
whispered.

Vernon got out of his rental car and walked

back to meet the police commissioner. "This isn't too cool," Frank whispered. "If DeCampo is caught setting up a media hatchet job . . ."

The two men met on the dock and started talking. Joe and Frank were too far away to hear any words, but they could see the angry gestures. Vernon glanced at his watch. DeCampo peered into the darkness at the edge of the dock—uncomfortably close to the Hardys.

"Looks like they're waiting for somebody else, who hasn't shown yet," Frank said. "Maybe there *is* a Mr. X behind all this."

Shrugging, Rod Vernon headed back to his car. DeCampo followed, still gesturing.

"They've been stood up," Joe said. "Maybe we should step right up and ask who they're waiting for."

He put one foot on the dock, but that was as far as he got.

The brown rental car burst into flames with a roar, a tongue of fire licking up from the trunk. Joe and Frank staggered back.

The two men on the dock, much closer to the blast, were flung headlong, trapped beside the blaze!

Chapter

7

FRANK AND JOE BOTH LEAPT into action, running full-tilt onto the dock. Vernon and DeCampo both lay unmoving. The rental car was burning uncontrollably, and parts of the wooden dock had caught fire, too.

"We've got to get them away from there!" Frank yelled.

Joe looked doubtfully at DeCampo's dead-white face. "What if he's bleeding internally? We could hurt him."

"If we leave him there and the gas tank goes up, it'll kill him for sure," Frank snapped.

Together, they struggled to drag the two men to safety. Once the injured men were out of direct danger, Joe ran for the van and its mobile phone.

"There's been an explosion on the docks," he reported to the emergency operator. "Two men have been injured—*seriously*."

He joined Frank in giving mouth-to-mouth resuscitation to the two men until an ambulance arrived. The shriek of its siren was a welcome sound, until the Hardys realized it was accompanied by a police car.

When the patrol officers recognized the two casualties, they were on the radio immediately. "You two just stand here," one officer said to the Hardys as her partner called headquarters. Joe noticed her hand hovering by the gun butt at her hip. This is going to be just great, he told himself.

A flood of police reinforcements arrived, red and blue lights flashing in the darkness and sirens screaming. The lead car's door flew open, and out stepped Parker Lawrence. "Just like in the TV cop shows," Joe muttered.

The acting chief marched up to Frank and Joe. "Want to explain what you're doing here?" he asked curtly.

Frank shrugged. "We were following Rod Vernon—as it turns out, to a secret meeting with Commissioner DeCampo."

"Ah—um-hm." Lawrence went from angry to poker-faced as this sank in.

"And then Vernon's car exploded." Frank was on safer ground here. "Obviously, someone planted a bomb to get Rod Vernon—" He paused for a second. "Maybe it was aimed at the commissioner, too."

Lawrence headed for his car. "Equally obviously, we have a strong suspect, someone who considered both men to be his enemies—Ezra Collig."

"Chief Collig?" Joe said in disbelief. "But he's not even here. Vernon arranged to switch cars, and Collig didn't know. He's probably still sitting in the parking lot at the TV station."

"That's a poor attempt to create an alibi—with friendly witnesses." Lawrence glared at them stonily. "You apparently found out about the switch. So could Collig. And I'm sure you know that there are lots of ways to set up a long-range explosion: timers, radio controls—"

He picked up the microphone from his car radio and called headquarters. "Dispatch a car to the WBPT station parking lot. Officers will take in custody a male in a black sedan—Ezra Collig. He's wanted for questioning in connection with the bomb attack on Rod Vernon and Commissioner DeCampo at the docks."

Lawrence hesitated. "Make sure the personnel are I.A. unit members."

Internal Affairs, Joe realized. He wants his own flunkies to arrest the chief.

"As for you," Lawrence went on, "you're coming to headquarters. I want statements from both of you, and then I'll decide whether to hold you as material witnesses."

The Hardys rode in the acting chief's police car—in the backseat, where usually only prisoners rode. At least, Joe thought, we aren't handcuffed.

They had almost reached headquarters when an urgent call came in on the car radio. "The chief—I mean, Ezra Collig wasn't in the parking lot."

Giving their statements to two detectives inside took only a few minutes, but Joe and Frank wasted a couple of hours in Bayport's police headquarters while Parker Lawrence decided what to do with them. Actually, he didn't spend much time thinking. He was too busy directing an intensive manhunt all over town.

As word of the bombing—and the search for Collig—spread, headquarters filled with media people.

When Joe and Frank were finally sent to Lawrence's office, they found him sweating. Joe noticed that the man's usually immaculate uniform was rumpled. This was his first test as acting chief. So far it appeared that Lawrence was fumbling the ball.

He took it out on the boys. "You two are finished on this case," he growled as they stood in front of his desk. "I don't want you getting in my way again."

"I don't see how keeping an eye on Vernon got in your way," Frank said.

"Some good your eye did him," Lawrence sneered. "Or the commissioner."

"If we hadn't been around, they'd probably have burned to death on that dock," Joe burst out. "You should have taken better care of Vernon if he was snitching for you."

"Just out of curiosity," Frank asked, "was DeCampo the one who came up with the idea of smearing Chief Collig? Or was it someone else?"

Lawrence stared stonily at him. Frank continued impatiently, "We know there was no love lost between Collig and DeCampo. We heard DeCampo threaten to fire him. What doesn't fit is that DeCampo and Vernon were obviously waiting for someone on the dock—someone who didn't show."

"I don't have time to listen to this!" Lawrence shouted. "We know who set the bomb— Collig! He proved it by running. He must know by now that we want to question him, and he hasn't surrendered himself."

He cut himself off and glared at the Hardys. When he spoke again, his voice was tighter and higher. "Maybe I should remind you that your father's license is hanging by a thread. If you want him to work again, butt out."

"Sure, we get it, your mind is made up, so you don't want anyone confusing you with facts," Joe said.

"*Out!*" was Lawrence's only reply.

* * *

It was early morning when Frank and Joe returned home. Their mother was up, on the phone with their father. "Looks like we won't have to call a lawyer to get the boys away from the police," Laura Hardy said. "They're walking in the door now."

"But we've got a real problem, Mom," Frank said. "You and Dad should know about it."

Picking up the phone, he gave a rundown of what had happened in the last couple of days, including Parker Lawrence's threats about Fenton's license. The room was silent when he finished.

Then Fenton said, "Put me on the speaker phone."

"I said I'd stake my reputation on Collig's being innocent," the boys' father said. "Now I'll have to risk my business. Frank, are you sure those two were waiting for someone?"

"That's the way it looked," Frank said.

"DeCampo was definitely looking for someone," Joe added.

"And if we don't do something, Collig is going to be railroaded into jail." Fenton Hardy paused for a moment. "I say go for it, guys." He laughed. "Not that I expect Lawrence to keep my license from me. I've got enough police friends in other towns—or states, for that matter. What do you think, Laura?"

She smiled. "I think you boys had better crack this case. I'd hate to move."

"Thanks, Mom—Dad." Joe was grateful for the vote of confidence, until he realized the size of the job facing him and Frank. How were they supposed to clear Ezra Collig?

After a few more moments of discussing strategy with their father, they hung up.

"I'm bushed," Joe said, yawning. "It's bed for—"

His words were cut off by the ringing of the phone.

"Now, who'd be calling us at this hour?" Laura Hardy said.

Frank picked up the phone to hear Chet Morton on the other end. "Hey, Frank," his old friend said. "I sure hope I didn't wake you, but there's something weird going on out here. Mom and Dad are away, so I'm holding down the fort alone. A little while ago I started hearing noises. I thought of calling the cops, but I'd hate to have it turn out to be a raccoon. Um—but I'd also hate to go out alone and have it turn out *not* to be a raccoon." Chet was trying to sound cool about the situation, but Frank could tell he was nervous.

"We'll come out and help you check around," Frank promised. "We're leaving now."

He turned to Joe. "No time for sleep. Something's gone bump in the night out at the Mortons'."

Joe used the high beams as they drove to the Morton farm. Chet and his family lived out where the real country began. There were no streetlights, but he easily spotted Chet's house. Every window was lit up.

"Glad you guys are here," Chet said, greeting the Hardys at the door.

"What kind of noises are you hearing?" Joe wanted to know.

"Shh! Listen!" Chet peered nervously into the darkness. Then they heard it, too.

Out of the inky night came a fuzzy crackling sound, followed by a sharp click.

"I've heard that before," Frank said. "Recently. But where?"

"Let's get some flashlights and check it out," Joe suggested. Armed with the lights and Chet's baseball bat, they set off across the barnyard. The sounds grew louder as they approached a small patch of forest not far from the road.

"Voices!" Chet burst out.

Frank sped up. "I think I know what this is!" He plunged into the woods, followed by the others. Cutting across the road, he found what he expected.

It was a black sedan, canted at a crazy angle. One wheel was up on a tree root, and the driver's door was open, as if the car had been abandoned quickly. With a blast of crackling static the police-band radio on the front seat came to life: "Headquarters—A-thirteen in position on River Road. No sign of fugitive. Over."

Then came a sharp click as the headquarters' radio operator responded.

"Well, now we know why Lawrence's manhunt was such a bust," Joe said. "Collig was listening in on every one of his orders."

It was only a couple of hours to sunrise when the Hardys found themselves back at police headquarters. Parker Lawrence was not pleased. Besides calling the cops about discovering the car, Joe and Frank had also informed WBPT, the *Bayport Times,* and a couple of radio stations.

Joe grinned at the media people crowding the headquarters lobby. They were having a fine old time with the fact that Collig the fox had so embarrassingly eluded Lawrence's hounds.

The acting chief completely forgot about the media people when he saw the Hardys. "I told you what I'd do if I found you meddling in this case!" he shouted.

"Since when is reporting an abandoned vehicle meddling?" Joe asked. "Especially when it was one you were searching for so hard?"

"Face it, Lawrence," Frank said as cameras and microphones zoomed in on him. "You're after the wrong man. Collig didn't set that bomb. You can't even pin a clear motive on him. We're going to Millerton tomorrow." He glanced at his watch. "I guess I mean today. And we're going to get to the bottom of this bribery story."

In the brief silence that followed, they heard a reporter saying, "This is Bayport Newsradio, live from police headquarters."

When he realized their confrontation was being broadcast live, Lawrence shut up and sent the boys home. They got a few hours' sleep, then, yawning, set off for Millerton.

"I don't get it," Joe complained as they pulled away. "We were pretty groggy by the time we got home. But I'm sure I'd have noticed the gas gauge reading empty."

"We'd better fill up before we get on the interstate," Frank said.

They headed for their usual gas station. Frank paid the cashier while Joe worked the self-service pump.

"That'll do it," Joe said, hanging up the hose. "We were almost bone-dry."

As he started to open the passenger door, a figure suddenly darted out from a patch of bushes nearby. Joe stood frozen as the figure dashed past him, through the open door, and into the van.

It was Chief Collig!

Chapter

8

"WHA-WHAT ARE YOU DOING?" an utterly dumb-founded Joe asked.

"And why are you doing it *here?*" Frank had arrived at the other door. He stared in dismay at their uninvited guest.

"That should be obvious. I'm getting a lift out of this burg." Ezra Collig was calm and confident as he took a seat in the rear of the van. "I caught your little run-in with Parker Lawrence on the radio late last night. I was grabbing a cup of coffee at a greasy spoon outside of town."

He shifted in his seat. "Like you guys, I realized I'd never be able to beat this bombing rap if I stayed in Bayport. Lawrence wants my head on a spike over the door of headquarters. I've got to find someone who can tell my side of the story about what happened in Millerton. That means going there. So, when I heard you two were heading that way, I walked back to town and figured I'd hitch a ride."

"How did you know we were going to be here?" Frank asked.

"Oh, I know where you and your dad stop to get gas," Collig said. "So I just made sure you'd need some. Sorry about that—I owe you for half a tank of super unleaded."

The boys continued to stare in complete disbelief. Why didn't he just get in the van at the house? Joe wondered. Maybe Collig was enjoying playing bad guy a little too much.

Collig gestured for them to get in the van. "Well, come on! If you're going to stand out there and stare with your mouths open, you're going to call attention to us." He glanced at the open doors. "And right now attention is not what I need."

Joe climbed aboard and so, reluctantly, did Frank. "You know, you could land us in trouble—deep trouble," Joe said at last. "I mean, officially you're a fugitive. How many times have you taken a dim view—"

"In other words, how many times have you done this to *me* over the years?" Collig interrupted. "You've just about driven me nuts, helping suspects escape, fouling up my investigations. Well, this time *I'm* the fugitive."

He looked at them pleadingly. "So, why can't

71

you butt in this once, when I really need your interference?"

"The people we've always helped have been innocent." The words had burst from Frank's mouth and surprised him almost as much as they did Joe. He glanced from Joe's shocked face to Collig's stony one. He took a deep breath before adding, "Okay. So I think you're innocent, too. Let's roll."

They pulled out of the gas station and headed for the interstate.

"A fugitive," Ezra Collig mused as they rolled along. "It's been a long time since I had to pull up stakes and run for it. Sharpens your mind a bit."

Frank wanted to ask what he meant, but the chief continued, paying no attention. "Since Bea passed away, I've just been living on the rebound, not really living, just reacting to things. It's funny. Hearing Lawrence order his stooges to pick me up was like a strong slap in the face. Wake up, Collig! You've got a life to take care of!"

Frank took the opportunity to ask some questions. "Maybe you can tell us some of the stuff that Lawrence hasn't found out yet," he said. "For instance, where did you spend those mystery months between your first job and coming to Bayport?"

Collig looked embarrassed. "It's no mystery,

really. All Lawrence had to do was check." His ears went red. "I was in high school."

"What?" Joe stared. He *couldn't* have heard that right!

"I was sweeping a store by day and taking night classes to get my high-school diploma." Collig became a little defensive as he explained, "It's not something I wanted spread all over."

"You were a high-school dropout?" Frank asked.

"You make that sound like the title of an old crime movie. You have to remember, things were a lot different when I was a kid." Collig grinned. "No, I'm not going to tell you about wrestling grizzly bears on the way to school. But in those days you could get a decent job even if you didn't finish school. And I don't mean flipping burgers." Collig's lips tightened. "Things were tough at home, and it was time for me to feed myself. I left school in the middle of my senior year. Got a job on a road-building crew."

He smiled at the memory. "It was backbreaking work. Then one day I happened to see an old chain-gang flick. The prisoners in the movie were doing the same work I was." He gave the boys another grin. "So I decided to change careers."

"And you became a cop?" Frank asked.

"The Millerton force didn't have the highest standards," Collig admitted. "If you had two arms, two legs, and enough muscle, you got the job. Being able to write your name was sort of like icing on the cake. It was a different world then, guys, a different world. . . ."

Frank decided to ask about something else that had been puzzling him. "Chief, did you recognize the picture that ran in the *Bayport Times?*"

"Believe it or not, that was me—a lot younger and much skinnier, of course." Collig patted his ample midsection as he spoke.

"I mean, do you remember the picture itself? Where it was taken?"

Collig shook his head, frowning. "There was just a brick wall behind me. Maybe if I saw the whole picture, it would shake a memory loose."

"The picture came to the *Times* by messenger, and it was cut in half," Joe added.

"Cut in half?" Collig sat a little straighter in his seat, a shadow flitting across his face. He shook his head. "Nope. That doesn't ring any bells."

"So how come you went back to school?" Joe asked.

"Ambition," Collig told him. "I wanted a better job as a cop. But I found out the better police forces had stiffer requirements—like a high-school diploma."

He shrugged, probably to chase away the remembrance of those past disappointments. "After getting turned down for the fifth time, I settled in Atlantic Heights, a bit down the coast from here, got a job to keep body and soul together, and enrolled in night school.''

"Why Atlantic Heights?" Frank asked.

"They have a good police force there, and the desk sergeant was friendly. He said if I got a diploma, he'd see about getting me a job.''

"So you got your diploma," Joe said.

Collig nodded. "Believe it or not, I was a straight-A student. Till then I'd never much cared about studying. But now I had a reason to work.''

He smiled at some scene many years distant. "A couple of reasons, actually. I made up my senior year and graduated from Atlantic Heights High. My name's right there in their records, and of course the information is in the records down at headquarters. Lawrence could have found out if he'd just looked." Collig frowned. "But he was too busy trying to prove I was doing something crooked.''

"Wait a second," Joe said, glancing back at the chief. "You said that after you graduated that sergeant was going to get you a job on the local force. What happened?''

Collig shrugged. "Another sergeant's nephew got the slot instead of me. I don't regret my stay in Atlantic Heights, though. I got my diploma, and there was a cute instructor, right out of teacher's college. Bea Cowan. She made me the happiest man in the world when she agreed to become Bea Collig.''

"You married your teacher?" Joe exclaimed. That's one way to get good grades, he thought to himself.

"Yup," Collig said happily. "I sent out applications to all the nearby towns. The Bayport P.D. asked me to come for an interview and liked what they saw. The rest, as they say, is history."

Frank glanced in the rearview mirror for a look at Collig as they reached the crest of a hill. "Well, that takes care of the time between leaving Millerton and reaching Bayport," he said. "Can you tell us about your first job? Your time in Millerton?"

They went over the top of the hill, and Joe suddenly leaned forward in his seat. "No more time for trips down memory lane," he said suddenly. "We've got major trouble up ahead."

Frank watched the road and became pale. The thin morning traffic was slowing and bunching up as they approached a barricade of police cars.

"A roadblock," he said, his throat dry. "And we've rolled right into it!"

Chapter

9

"IT'S MY OWN STUPID FAULT." Collig's expression was grim as he peered through the windshield. "I was busy yakking instead of thinking."

He growled low in his throat as the van joined the tail end of the line of cars waiting to pass through. "The force has a standard plan for setting up roadblocks. Know who picked this place? Me. I figured right beyond the crest of this hill was perfect—fugitives wouldn't see the roadblock until it was too late."

"Right—just as the cops would see us now if we tried to turn around. It would be like waving a big red flag saying, 'Come and chase us!'" Joe glanced at his brother. "We've got a problem. What do we do?"

"We're in plain view of everyone," Collig

said unhappily. "Even if I bail out, the boys will see me—and they'll know which vehicle I left."

"That's true." In his mind's eye Frank just saw his father's P.I. license fly away.

"I don't suppose we could just ram our way through," Joe suggested.

"Right. No one would notice that." Frank gave his brother an annoyed look.

"I say, just hang tough." Collig left the seat he'd been in, moving to the shadows in the rear of the van.

If the cops open the back door, we've had it, Frank thought, but he didn't have much choice. They'd reached the barricade.

The police officer who approached them had a vaguely familiar face. Frank must have seen him around town. Certainly he recognized Frank. A big grin spread over the patrolman's round face. "Well, well, if it isn't the famous Hardy brothers! Making your trip to Millerton, I presume, as announced on the media."

Frank's insides froze. What if Parker Lawrence had decided to stop them? What if he'd issued orders to have them picked up? The van might well have become Chief Collig's limousine to jail!

Wild thoughts of escape flashed through Frank's mind. Then he realized that the officer was laughing. "You guys did a nice job of making Lawrence look like a twit. It was all over the morning news. Keep up the good work in Millerton. Pass on!''

The officer waved them through. ''See you on TV!''

Both Hardys breathed deep sighs of relief. The general dislike for Parker Lawrence in the Bayport force had rescued them! They continued down the interstate.

Behind them they heard dry laughter as Chief Collig returned to his seat. ''Well, we lucked out on that,'' he said.

''Let's hope our luck holds,'' Frank responded. ''I'm too young to die of a heart attack.''

''There shouldn't be any more roadblocks. That was the farthest location I ever planned.'' He paused for a second, then said casually, ''You didn't happen to get the badge number of the officer who let you through?''

''Why?'' Joe asked. ''Do you want to thank him?''

''No,'' Collig replied. ''If—*when* I get this mess cleared up, I intend to chew that cop out for letting me escape.''

The ride to Millerton took a couple of hours. At first Collig was quiet, having been jolted out of his talkative mood by the near-miss at the roadblock.

Gradually, though, Frank managed to start a conversation again, bringing it around to Collig's days in Millerton. Still, he never worked up the courage to ask Collig outright about the bribery charge. That seemed to be pushing it.

Collig had a huge fund of stories from what he called his rookie days. Some were funny, like when he got fooled into buying ice cream for a supposedly lost little girl. He found out the kid pulled that trick on every new cop who pounded the beat. "She should have weighed a ton from all the ice cream she put away," the chief said.

There were also scary stories such as the first time he'd had to pull his gun. After chasing a burglar for six blocks, the guy turned on him with a knife. "We faced off for a long moment," Collig said. "That stupid switchblade looked like a sword to me. As it turned out, my gun must have looked like a cannon to him because he gave up, and I got my first collar—my first arrest."

Frank felt as if he was getting a peek into another world—one out of the past. "It's all different now," Collig said. "Criminal law and how it's enforced have changed completely. When I started out, there was a lot less hassle about using deadly force. Using a gun in certain situations would have won a promotion and a medal in the old days. Now it would get you thrown off the force. We didn't have to knock and announce ourselves as police when we raided a place. And the idea of reading a card to warn a crook of his rights . . ." He just shook his head.

"Back in those days if you didn't like some

character's looks, you could stop him on the street and toss him. Search his pockets. Today that would be 'unreasonable search and seizure' because I didn't have 'sufficient cause.' When a known thief turned up on your beat, you'd whack the guy in the calf with your nightstick.''

"Just to scare him?" Joe asked.

"No, as crime prevention. If the guy's leg hurt so bad he couldn't run, he couldn't steal." Collig shrugged. "Sooner or later the thief would get the message. He'd grow tired of getting whacked and move along."

"What did the public think about this?" Frank wondered out loud.

"Most of them thought it was great. Store owners on the beat would give you presents. I knew one officer who brought a little red wagon along on his beat every Christmas. It would be piled high by the end of the day. Restaurants and diners were happy to have cops around for protection. They'd let us in 'on the arm.' We ate for free."

"Chet Morton would sign up for a chance like that," Joe joked.

"Some guys took advantage, of course. My old partner would take the freshest fruit off stands without paying. He wouldn't even ask." A frown passed over Collig's face as he spoke. For the next few miles he was silent.

"What's the matter, Chief?" Frank finally asked. "Something wrong?"

"I was just reminded of something else," Collig said, then added, "the blue wall of silence."

"What was that?" Joe wanted to know.

"If a cop did something wrong, it was settled inside the department, in secrecy. No press releases, no snooping reporters. No one ever wanted the force or any cop to look bad."

Is that what happened to the chief? Frank wondered. Did he do something wrong—something halfway okay in that simpler world but illegal in today's world?

"Sounds as if you had some kind of problem with that wall." Frank hoped he could get Collig to talk about it. Then maybe they wouldn't have anything to investigate in Millerton.

"You could say that," Collig grunted. But that was all he said. He simply sat, tense and silent, for the rest of the ride. Frank knew he still couldn't ask the chief about the bribery charge.

"Just drop me off here," Collig said abruptly as they came to a hill at the edge of town. Frank got his first view of Millerton—a vista of low brick buildings. "I don't believe it," Collig said. "The place has hardly changed."

"Do you want to arrange a place to meet—"

Before Frank could even finish, Collig had jumped out of the van and disappeared into the bushes. He didn't even look back.

Shaking his head, Frank drove into the center of town.

"Why didn't you just ask him about the bribery thing?" Joe wanted to know.

"Why didn't you?" Frank answered.

Joe shrugged, and they both understood it was a question they couldn't ask Collig directly.

"Where to first?" Joe asked.

"Let's try the library. They should have back issues of the local newspapers."

An overworked librarian was not very happy at their request. "I'll have to unlock the Special Document Room for you. The papers from that far back are kept in bound volumes there."

"No microfilm?" Frank said, surprised.

"We keep hoping to get it in the budget, but this is a poor town." A glance around the library confirmed that. Its dingy walls should have been painted years before, there were gaps in the shelves of books, and a lot of the stock seemed to be badly dog-eared paperbacks.

The Special Documents Room turned out to be an airless closet down in the basement. Sighing, Joe took the volume covering the year before Collig's resignation. Frank got down the volume covering the year after.

After a few hours of fruitless searching, Joe closed his book. "There's not a mention, not even a hint, of any police problems. All they were interested in was how the new interstate would revitalize the area's economy."

"I guess they were wrong about that, too." Frank thought of the tired-looking town as he shut his book. "I've covered more than a year after Collig left, and there's no mention of bribery."

"Maybe this was settled behind the blue wall of silence," Joe suggested, "without press releases."

Frank nodded. "Without snooping reporters, either, I bet." He stretched, then returned the volumes to their shelves. "Well, let's try to pierce that blue wall—at police headquarters."

After asking the librarian for directions, the Hardys jumped in their van and drove off.

Millerton Police Headquarters was a smoke-stained brick building, as shabby as the rest of the town. Frank noticed litter tossed around the front steps as they walked in. "We're here to see Detective Preznowski," he told the officer behind the scarred front desk.

A phone call to their father had set the police old-boy system to work. Out came Detective Dwight Preznowski, a short, rotund man. "Come on in here," he said, leading them to an empty squad room. "A pal of mine in Junction City owes your dad, and I owe him. I sat here and waited for you guys, and you made me miss a free lunch—the shoo-flies from Bayport were buying."

"Shoo-flies?" Joe asked.

"That's what we call Internal Affairs people," Preznowski explained. "You know the song— 'Shoo, fly, don't bother me.' "

"So, the Bayport Internal Affairs people are here?" Frank said.

"Yeah, asking questions about Collig and all this ancient history as if it happened two days ago. They're taking us out to lunch to 'ensure our cooperation.' Instead, I'm giving you all that they got." Preznowski walked to a nearby desk, scooped up a thin file folder, and handed it to Frank.

"This is it? His service record?" Frank scanned the two sheets inside. Height, weight—had Ezra Collig ever been that thin? Here was the date Collig had joined the force, his commendations, arrests, and after less than a year, his resignation. The second sheet was a typed resignation letter, painfully citing personal reasons.

"Not very much," Joe said, reading over his brother's shoulder.

Preznowski shrugged. "It's all we've got on paper."

Frank turned back to the first sheet, remembering one of Collig's stories on the ride. "Can you get us the file on"—he checked the record for the name of Collig's partner—"Raymond Bozeman?"

Sighing, Preznowski disappeared into a file room. Soon he was back, with a somewhat thicker file. "Happy?"

"We'll see." Frank ran through the file, scanning dates, commendations, arrests, partners—

the last being Ezra Collig. Then he found a resignation letter, dated about a month after Collig's.

"Personal reasons again," Joe said.

"Is there a listing of people who left the force around this time?" Frank asked.

It took some digging, but in the end the Hardys had a list of seven names, which they checked against the files.

"One medical discharge, one retirement, and five resignations, starting with Collig's."

Frank raised his eyebrows at Joe. "All of them for personal reasons."

Chapter

10

STANDING BY HIS BATTERED DESK in the squad room, Detective Preznowski stared in grudging admiration at the list the Hardys had compiled. "In a couple of hours you two kids have managed to accomplish more than those shoo-flies did in the last few days."

He rattled the paper in his hand. "Come on. Let's go talk to the chief." He led Frank and Joe down a corridor to an office marked Chief.

Chief Gilmartin of the Millerton police force was a thin, wiry man with a fringe of white hair over his ears. Frank saw that the man's faded blue eyes stayed sharply on Preznowski as the detective related his story.

"We've had reporters and those Internal Affairs types from Bayport all over here,"

Gilmartin said. "But this is the first solid lead anyone has come up with."

Frank felt a twinge. Was it a solid lead that might lead Collig into more trouble?

"The Bayport I.A. guys are more like accountants than cops," the chief went on. "They have no idea how to dig into a case. Would you believe that they were trying to find records of disciplinary hearings? From *those* days? None of that went down on paper."

Obviously, Frank thought, Chief Gilmartin was a graduate of the blue-wall-of-silence school.

"Were you on the force when Collig was here?" Frank asked.

The chief shook his head. "That was a little before my time. I came on to replace one of the guys on this list." He tapped the paper.

"When I started pounding the beat, a lot of the local shopkeepers were angry at us. They didn't trust the police. And the chief back then, Old Man McClure, set up all new rules. 'No officer shall accept any gratuities,' " he quoted. "I remember, I had to look up what a gratuity was. Why couldn't he have just said, 'no tips'? A lot of guys were nervous. Nobody wanted to talk about why new rules were needed."

He shrugged. "You didn't need to be a great detective to figure some guys must have been shaking down the local merchants. But the stink died down pretty fast. Nobody likes to remember that kind of thing."

"Would it be possible to track down the men who resigned?" Frank asked.

Chief Gilmartin shook his head. "Not from our records. How long were they here? Five, seven—the longest service was ten years. Back then you didn't get a pension till you put in twenty-five years. There was no reason for us to keep track of these guys."

"How about retirees?" Frank suggested desperately. "Maybe some of them would remember exactly what happened."

The chief reached into his desk and came out with a list. "You can make a copy of this. I gave one to the Bayport Internal Affairs guys." Gilmartin didn't look very hopeful. "Some of the men from those days are dead. The rest are all over the Sun Belt. When you're old, winter in Millerton isn't much fun."

Frank scanned the list. He saw addresses in Florida, Arizona, California. "Have the Bayport investigators contacted any of these people?"

"Not on our phones," Gilmartin said firmly. "Money is tight around here. I heard one of them say they could wait till they got back to their office to make the calls."

The Hardys nodded. That fit in with the way Parker Lawrence wanted the case investigated—nice and slow.

"Isn't there anyone in town who might know about that time?" Frank asked.

"Maybe Commissioner Potts," Preznowski

suggested. "The Commish was around in those days."

"The police commissioner?" Joe asked eagerly.

"Ah—no." Chief Gilmartin looked as if his detective had told a joke in very poor taste. "Some of our people call Potts 'Commissioner' as a joking nickname. He's an old, retired officer. A good cop, but I don't think he'd be of much use to you." Gilmartin continued to give Preznowski the evil eye.

"Well, sir, I guess we've taken up enough of your time." Frank was eager to get out of the office before he ran into any of the Bayport investigators. So far they'd been lucky. He also wanted one peek in the records to find out where Potts called home.

A brief search of Millerton's streets led them to the address they'd gotten from the files. Leonard Potts lived in a shabby apartment house on the poor side of a poor town. The Hardys had a shock when the apartment door opened. A raw-boned man with an unshaved chin peered out at them. His body was twisted, one hip leading the other.

"What can I do for you?" he asked.

"I'm Frank Hardy, and this is my brother, Joe. We're looking into something that happened in the police force about thirty-five years ago. Maybe you can help us."

"I was heading out for a little dinner," Potts told them. "You can come along and talk." He set off painfully down the stairs. Frank and Joe followed.

They went to a smoky little restaurant with a long bar down one side. "This place used to be Minty's, a cop hangout," Potts told them. "I still come in for old times' sake." He pointed to the exposed brick wall, where a moth-eaten moose head hung. "We had a regular tradition. All the rookies had their pictures taken with their partner and the moose head. We used to say it looked like Chief McClure." A waitress came, and Potts ordered soup and salad without glancing at the menu. The boys asked for hamburgers. They had missed their lunch.

Potts watched them from his chair. "I guess you notice I go off at an odd angle these days," he said. "I was the longest-service, most-decorated cop on the force. Then one day my partner and I went to check on a stolen car. Punk inside had a nine-millimeter pistol. Killed my partner, put four bullets into me. They did a job on my hip and spine. I came out of the hospital, and they gave me a medal. Told me I could work at headquarters—easy duty.

"Then, one day, I had to go down to the firing range. Somebody shot his gun, and I was under a table, screaming. The force had a big problem—a hero with a medal who couldn't stand guns. They called it a nervous breakdown, gave me a medical discharge. I'm fine—as long as I remember to take my pills."

He took a little box out of his pocket. "Pink, white, blue." Potts washed down each pill with a sip of water. Then he looked at them with red-rimmed eyes.

"So," he said. "What do you want to know about the Millerton police force?"

He started nodding when he heard their story. "Yeah, yeah, I remember those days." He gave them a lopsided grin. "Even if I say so myself, I was a pretty good cop. I had a nose for every-thing happening on my beat. So I noticed when the shop owners began acting funny—something between hate and fear."

Potts frowned. "I remember getting a meal on the arm, and the diner owner coming out and sounding off about it. 'Isn't it enough that I pay you guys off?' he said. 'Do you have to eat me out of house and home?' " Potts shifted in his seat. "Of course, it turned out to be Bozeman."

"Raymond Bozeman?" Joe asked.

The old man nodded. "He was quite the lad, Ray Bozeman. Everyone expected him to move up when Sergeant Henried retired, because everyone took Bozeman's orders already. But he was too greedy, making money on the side—protection money. Stores began getting windows broken or maybe they'd have a little legal trou-ble. Bozeman would step in, and then everything was fine."

Potts leaned back, eyes half-closed as he remembered. "Bozeman had a rookie partner.

Every Friday the kid went out, regular as clock-work, to collect the money from the store owners."

The food had arrived, but neither Hardy was hungry now. "Do you remember the rookie's name?" Frank asked. If Potts actually fingered Ezra Collig—

Potts shrugged. "Who can recall after all those years? He was only around a couple of months. Then he left. After that, Bozeman and a bunch of other guys resigned."

Frank and Joe paid the bill, leaving the old man to his soup and salad. "Did I help?" Potts asked.

"You answered a lot of *my* questions," Frank said. But I don't happen to like the answers, he thought.

"I still don't believe it," Joe said as they stepped into the darkening street. "A rookie who was making collections, then was the first to leave the force. We know who it has to be. But why—*how* did he wind up doing that?"

"Boys!" a voice hissed from a nearby alley.

The Hardys turned to see Ezra Collig beckoning them.

"That place you were in—is it still Minty's?" Collig asked when they'd joined him. They shook their heads. "It used to be a cop hangout. I thought some of the old gang might be there."

"Gang?" Frank said a little coldly. "What an interesting word. There was no 'gang' in there,

Chief. Just an old man named Potts. He told us about Ray Bozeman and his rookie partner. Oh, yes, and there was also something about extortion and collecting protection money from local merchants.''

Collig focused on the ground. "I know all about that," he said quietly. "I was the bagman."

Joe and Frank stood silent for a second. They'd been convinced by Potts's story, but actually hearing Chief Collig confess shook them up.

"Wait! You have to hear the whole story!" When Collig raised his eyes, they were wild. "I was just a kid—"

"Oh, no," Joe said, "not the old 'I was just a kid' cop-out."

Collig glared at him. "I was a raw rookie, just off the farm, and I got chosen as partner by the hottest cop on the force. Ray Bozeman taught me how to be a cop. I thought he was the greatest guy in the world. When he asked me to take over the collections for the Policemen's Fund, of course I did."

He shook his head at his own stupidity. "I couldn't understand why all the storekeepers seemed so angry at donating to a charity fund. Finally one shopkeeper's daughter exploded at me. 'I thought you were a pretty good guy,' she said. 'Why are you helping to rob my father?' ''

The chief's mouth quirked in a self-mocking

smile. "That's when I learned the Policemen's Fund was mainly a charity for one policeman—Ray Bozeman. He got most of the take and split the rest with his pals.

"I was sick to realize the racket I was involved with. And I was scared, too. How could I go up against Bozeman and his boys? Police work is dangerous enough with a partner to cover your back. When you're fighting crooks in front and can't trust the guys behind—well, it's like being caught in a cross fire. You don't survive."

He sighed. "It was the toughest thing I ever did, but I took my bag of collections straight to Chief McClure. The old man nearly swallowed his dentures, but you have to give him credit. He believed me and promised the situation would be taken care of."

"What happened to you?" Joe asked.

"The chief told me that by turning Bozeman in, I'd turned myself into a target. He's the one who suggested I get out of town. I stayed in touch until I heard that Bozeman and his cronies had left the force. Then I thought the nightmare was over."

"And?"

"And I got on with my life. I tried to get a better job, discovered I needed more education. Then I met Bea. She showed me I could be more than a cop on the beat. I even went to college, got a degree, won promotions. . . ." His voice ran down. "My decision to turn that money in was the turning point that set the whole course of my life. You could say it made me the man I am today."

He looked down at his hands. "Now Bea's dead, and this accusation from my past has surfaced. The mistake I thought I had set right . . . there's no one left who knows the *whole* story. Chief McClure died years ago. He was proud to see where I'd gotten. And Captain Frazee, he knew the score, too, but a heart attack took him a dozen years back."

Frank nodded thoughtfully. "There's no written proof, because they didn't keep records about dirty cops."

"I have no proof of my story at all," Collig said quietly.

"Maybe we could talk with Potts again," Joe began, turning back toward the street.

His words were cut off by three gunshots—and a wild scream.

Chapter

11

JOE AND FRANK RAN out of the alley toward the sound of the shots—into the street. They found it empty. Apparently, Joe thought, people in this neighborhood didn't gather to see what was going on when they heard gunfire. No, very sensibly they stayed away.

Wait—the street wasn't completely empty. Joe spotted a huddled figure lying in the gutter. "Frank! Over here!"

Together they raced toward the man in the gutter.

A dark figure leaned out of an alley farther down the block. "Down!" Frank yelled, catching a glint of light on a gun barrel. Four more shots blasted out.

The Hardys hit the ground. Across the street

from them the prone figure let out another wild scream.

"I don't get it," Joe whispered. "Those shots are going way over him. Why—"

Frank had rolled behind a parked car. Rising to a crouch, he dashed from car to car, using every scrap of cover. He peered into the darkness of the alley where the gunman had been.

"You can get up, Joe. The shooter's gone."

An infuriated roar came from the alley they had left. "Are you two out of your minds, running into gunfire like that? You could have been killed!" Collig shouted.

Frank was across the street and kneeling over the crumpled form in the street. "I thought that baggy coat looked familiar," Joe said, joining his brother.

It was Leonard Potts. He lay on his side, all his muscles tensed, his body pulled into a tight ball.

"He doesn't seem to be hit," Frank said, reaching down to touch the man. Potts flinched. The sound that burst from his throat was the whimper of a frightened animal.

"The gunshots!" Joe said in a hushed voice. "They must have set him off again."

Chief Collig joined the boys, staring down. "Len?" he said in shock. "Len Potts?"

For a second the tensed figure on the ground coiled. Potts's lids opened, his eyes not focusing completely as they took in Collig, and he gasped. "Young Collig! Another ghost trying to kill me!"

"Another ghost?" Collig repeated. "What do you mean? What ghost? Who? You've got to tell me, Potts!"

The other man had curled himself into a ball again, a thin whine escaping from his teeth.

Collig turned in desperation to the Hardys. "Did you see the guy who was shooting? What do you think Potts meant?"

"He was just a shadow with a gun," Joe said.

"I have no idea what Potts is trying to say." Frank shook his head, staring at the helpless bundle Potts had become. "I'll tell you one thing, though. The only guy left who knew anything about Bozeman's extortion scheme won't be telling anyone about it soon."

The wail of sirens approached them through the streets.

"Can you tell us anything more about Bozeman?" Frank asked. He turned and found that Collig had disappeared.

Joe followed Frank's surprised gaze. "I guess we shouldn't be surprised," Joe said. "There are lots of alleys around here. And what do you expect a fugitive to do when he hears sirens?"

The Millerton police were the first to arrive. "Hey, it's the Commish!" one of the officers cried. He knelt to check the frail old man's pulse. "It's okay, pal. It's okay."

He turned to the Hardys. "What happened?"

"Somebody fired a gun from that alley over there," Joe said, pointing.

"Someone shot at Commissioner Potts?" the cop said in disbelief.

"We don't know. He was on the ground, but he wasn't hit."

"What kind of sicko would do a thing like that? Everybody around here knows the Commish. Nobody would want to hurt him."

"It looks like somebody was really aiming for his weak point." Joe's face was grim in the revolving red lights of an ambulance that had just arrived. Attendants in white coats were gently shifting Potts onto an ambulance gurney.

Frank turned to the patrolman, who was taking statements on his notepad. "Could you put us in touch with Detective Preznowski?"

Back at headquarters the Hardys stood with Preznowski in a now-crowded squad room. "So you say the Commish actually remembered a little about what happened way back when, huh? What do you know."

"According to Potts, Ray Bozeman was running an extortion racket," Frank said.

"Well, he sure doesn't sound like a model officer," Preznowski said. "So, what do you want?"

"We'd like more information on Bozeman. Maybe you can use your computer to check state records."

"Not now," Preznowski said. "The operator's gone for the day."

Frank lowered his voice. "If you can get me to the computer, *I* can get the information in a couple of minutes."

Preznowski unlocked a tiny room down the hall, where a nearly obsolete computer sat humming. "All I ask is that you don't break the machinery and give a copy of whatever you find to Chief Gilmartin."

Joe watched as Frank took a couple of minutes to get a feel for the machine. "Can you get this to do what we need?"

"Watch." Frank's fingers danced over the keyboard. "Okay. We're into the state data bases." It took a while, but they finally received a fairly complete report on Ray Bozeman's career.

"After he left Millerton, Bozeman got a few more jobs as a cop." Joe scanned through the printout.

"Right," Frank said. "I got that from the state law-enforcement records. I guess lots of small towns would be happy to hire an experienced lawman."

Joe read a little farther down. "Ah. Fired for running various scams. Then he got dirtier and dirtier, until he completely went over to the other side. Convictions for armed robbery—this guy is getting more violent. Then he tried to knock over a bank, got nailed, and caught eight to ten years in the state pen. Where did this stuff come from? The crime and court data banks?''

Frank nodded. ''The hot info is at the bottom. I got that from the Corrections Bureau computer. According to them, Bozeman was released a couple of months ago. But when I accessed the parole authority records, guess who hasn't been visiting his parole officer lately? If you came up with the initials R. B., you wouldn't be wrong.''

Joe carefully folded up their copy of the printout. ''So, we've got the guy who headed that extortion ring all those years ago. Now he's out there somewhere. The question is, where?''

''We've got a whole lot of 'wheres' to wonder about,'' Frank pointed out. ''Where's Collig, for instance?''

Joe gave his brother a troubled glance. ''Do you believe his version of the extortion story?''

''I could go either way,'' Frank admitted. ''The facts we know support either case. Nothing's on paper. One thing I'm sure of, though. Collig did *not* try to blow Vernon and DeCampo up.''

''Why—'' Joe began, then he nodded. ''Sure. Maybe it was the same guy we got a glimpse of—the one trying nighttime target practice on Potts.''

''Unless, of course, Potts had a deadly enemy who just happened to send a bunch of bullets past him right after he talked with us.'' Frank shut down the computer. "But I think that's stretching coincidence too far."

They stopped by the squad room to thank Detective Preznowski and to leave a copy of their printout. The detectives in the room were wearing old, cheap, baggy suits. Joe could understand that. His dad used to warn about detecting in good clothes. "Wear a good suit, and you're bound to get mud, crud, or blood on it," he'd say. "Only cops who stay in offices can dress up for the job."

That's why Joe immediately noticed the two men in better-grade suits who came rushing over to snatch up the paper. One, a tall guy wearing a high-fashion suit, looked like an ugly version of Parker Lawrence. The man's hair was cut in the same style as the acting chief's, but he didn't have the same telegenic face. His lantern jaw jutted out as he started reading.

They say imitation is the sincerest form of flattery, Joe thought. This is one ambitious cop.

The other man was short and pudgy, sport jacket open with a sweater stretching over his swelling belly. With his chipmunk cheeks and tiny forehead, he looked like the perfect sidekick, Joe thought.

The guy sounded the part, too. "So who's this Bozeman?" the chubby guy asked, reading the printout.

"He was on the first list these two turned up," Lantern Jaw said impatiently. "Collig's partner, remember? So, he turned out to be a crook. Maybe the boss—''

Sure, Lawrence will find some way to use that to smear Collig some more, Joe thought bitterly.

Preznowski spoke up. "Since you gentlemen already know the Hardys, it's only fair that I introduce you to them. This is Detective Spratt''— he pointed to the tall man—"and Detective Pickerell.''

"Keep up the good work, guys.'' Joe turned to his brother. "Let's blow this joint.''

In their van again the boys were silent until they were out of the Millerton city limits.

"Did you get a load of those two clowns?'' Joe finally said. "They can't really be detectives. They'd look more at home behind the counter at Mr. Pizza.''

"Nope,'' Frank objected. "Tony would hire brighter help.'' He steered the car onto the interstate and upped the speed. "I'm not worried about them, but this case is getting to me. Especially since everything we learned in Millerton— except what Collig told us—only makes him look worse.''

Behind them a car came roaring up. Frank glanced in the rearview mirror, only to see an old, tan station wagon gaining on them.

"We'll let this guy pass—whoa!''

The passenger-side window of the station wagon was open as it swooped past. A hand appeared, and Frank and Joe both stared to see what it held: a bundle of waxy sticks with a sputtering fuse!

"Holy—" Joe gasped.

The hand let go of the dynamite—tossing it right in the path of the Hardys' van!

Chapter

12

HIS FACE PALE, eyes glued to the bundle of destruction bouncing on the road, Frank Hardy swerved the van wildly, giving it gas. Whoever threw the dynamite figured nicely, he thought. We're almost on top of it, and the fuse is almost gone. Unless we get around it fast—

The front wheels of the van almost hit the waxy sticks as he steered. He goosed the gas pedal, trying to put as much distance between them and the dynamite as possible.

The road curved, but Frank and Joe still saw the blast behind them. They felt it, too. The force of the explosion hit the van as if a giant hand kicked the rear bumper. The extra speed sent them screaming through the curve, nearly toppling.

Frank fought the wheel as they skidded. He was flung hard enough against his seat belt to bruise his shoulder, but he managed to steer into the skid and, with just inches of roadway to spare, regain control of the van.

Shakily he drove to the shoulder of the road and stopped the vehicle.

"N-nice job," Joe finally managed to say.

"Do we have a small crowbar in the back?" Frank asked. "I think I need help prying my fingers off the wheel."

In moments, however, he was turning the key to start the van up again.

"Hey, you're not going to try to catch the Mad Bomber of Route I-forty-nine, are you?" Joe asked.

"No, but I'd like to put some space between us and that bit of do-it-yourself road work. I hear sirens in the distance. I think Millerton's Finest will be getting tired of finding us at the scene of all the weirdness." They left as fast as the law allowed.

"I don't get it," Joe complained as they drove along the interstate. "We go to Millerton, and first somebody shoots at us, then someone throws a bomb."

"I think that's the same somebody," Frank said. "Either that or the Millerton Tourist Board has a real problem."

"What I mean is, what did we do to deserve

all that attention? We found a list of other cops who quit the force. Then we dug up one of the walking wounded, who told us about the extortion scheme and talked as if Chief Collig were a crook. And we got some info on Ray Bozeman.''

''You could write a great paragraph on 'How We Spent Our Day,' '' Frank told him.

''My point is, that's hardly enough to make someone try to kill us,'' Joe insisted. ''We must have learned something we don't realize.''

''Okay, let's go over it again. What places did we visit? The library, police headquarters, Potts's apartment, that restaurant, an alley, headquarters again. Oh!'' he suddenly exclaimed, banging his fist against the steering wheel. ''We must have been deaf and blind. Collig mentioned the place. Potts actually *told* us. And we didn't catch it.''

''What?'' Joe asked.

''The restaurant we were in. What did it used to be called?''

''Minty's,'' Joe remembered. ''It used to be a cop hangout.''

''Where they had a tradition of taking pictures of new recruits and their partners standing by that moose head. It looked like the old chief, Potts told us, and even pointed to the stuffed head. *Which is hung from a brick wall.* Get it?''

''The picture of Collig that came to the *Bayport Times!*'' Joe exclaimed. ''It was cut from a larger one." He glanced at his brother. "You think it was a picture of Bozeman?"

"It was something that somebody was afraid would be recognized. And that opens up all sorts of possibilities." Frank frowned over the steering wheel. "For one thing it explains the attacks. What did we learn about on this trip? Bozeman. Suppose Bozeman saw we were getting a little too close to identifying him. We spent a long time at headquarters. Then we went to see Potts. And where did we go next? Minty's! Yeah, I can see Bozeman getting a little nervous. So, he decides to put a scare into Potts to shut him up."

"Maybe he didn't know that Potts has a fear of gunshots," Joe said.

"Or maybe he did." Frank looked grim. "Anyway, we turn up, and he sends a few shots at us, as a warning. But we go back to the police station. So he decides we need to be shut up— permanently."

"Either Bozeman is very shy or he's a nut," Joe said.

"Well, you might be shy, too, if you were the source of those corruption accusations."

Frank glanced over his shoulder. "Let's try this on for size. Ever since we saw Collig and DeCampo fight, we've kind of suspected DeCampo was the one behind the smear campaign. Neither Lawrence nor Vernon seemed to be running things. DeCampo is a born organizer—he ran a great reform campaign. And he had a motive.''

Joe nodded, following Frank's argument.

"Suppose we were wrong. Suppose the smear campaign didn't start with DeCampo. He officially suspended Collig and started Lawrence's investigation the day after the accusations. What if he only jumped on a bandwagon that was already rolling? DeCampo was furious at Collig, and along comes this newsman with a story that might get Collig fired. Vernon would do DeCampo's political dirty work. And DeCampo would even be on TV, fighting corruption.''

"So, you're saying DeCampo didn't start the ball rolling," Joe said. "Vernon did.''

"Actually, Bozeman did," Frank explained. "He probably contacted Vernon with his own version of the bagman story.''

"Nice theory," Joe said. "I can only spot a few dozen holes. How come Bozeman waited all these years?''

"First, he was in jail, and then he probably lost track of Collig. But when the chief got that top cop award a few months ago, he got nationwide publicity." A slow smile spread over Frank's lips. "In fact, most of the stories referred to the fact that he was the only honest man in a corrupt administration. I wouldn't be surprised if that's what gave Bozeman the idea to smear him.''

"The sweetest revenge—I can buy that.'' Joe

nodded. "But how did Bozeman find us, to cause all this trouble in Millerton?"

Frank shrugged. "He followed us from Bayport. It's no secret we were going to Millerton. Remember how that cop kidded us? Our trip was announced on live radio. All Bozeman had to do was stake out our house until we left."

"But why us?" Joe insisted.

"Because he's scared of us," Frank said. "We turned up on the scene when DeCampo and Vernon were nearly killed. We said the chief was innocent. We were going to Millerton to find out the whole story."

"That bombing is the part that puzzles me," Joe said. "If Bozeman wanted to smear Collig, he needed Vernon and DeCampo. Why blow them up?"

"I think I've got an answer for that, too," Frank replied. "When did the blast happen? After public opinion began swinging over to Collig's side. Editorials were demanding that Vernon reveal his source. If Bozeman came out of the shadows, he wouldn't be a mystery man with dirt on the chief. He'd be identified, and Lawrence—and the media—would check his background. He might even be discredited if it was discovered that he'd led the extortion ring. But if Collig's accusers were murdered, who would be blamed?"

"Collig," Joe said grimly. "It all makes a twisted kind of sense." He glanced at Frank.

"I'll tell you something—if Bozeman has to be this devious, there's still something fishy about his story. I'd say it's a strong bet that Collig told the truth about being an innocent pawn in Bozeman's schemes."

He sighed. "Well, Frank, you've got a real theory. The only problem is, will we be able to get anyone to listen to it?"

They drove on to Bayport and straight to police headquarters. Luck was with them. Acting Chief Lawrence was still in the building when they arrived.

"What do you two want?" he demanded after they knocked on his office door.

"Have your people sent you the new information from Millerton?" Frank asked. "The stuff about the extortion ring?"

Lawrence nodded. "It looks like Collig was involved in dirtier business than we imagined."

"More men than Chief Collig were involved," Frank said. "For instance, there was Ray Bozeman. We have information that says he actually led the ring." He glanced over at Lawrence. "I don't suppose you know who started all the accusations?"

"Rod Vernon," Lawrence said impatiently.

"I mean, who told *him?*"

"I—ah, don't know." Lawrence seemed more than a little uncomfortable.

"Then perhaps you should consider this." Frank began laying out his whole theory of Bozeman as the original—and possibly lying—source of the story.

Lawrence was unconvinced.

"Well? Don't you see?" Joe burst out at the acting chief's doubtful expression. "If Bozeman is so worried about being discovered, it means he has something to hide—something more than the extortion ring. I think this means Chief Collig told us the truth. He was duped into collecting money for Bozeman."

"That's an interesting theory, but the facts still point to Ezra Collig." Lawrence wasn't about to change his mind. "Wait a minute! How could Collig have told you about his connection with Bozeman? You only found out about that in Millerton."

His eyes narrowed into angry slits. "Unless you saw him there—consorting with a fugitive, probably aiding him . . ." He leapt to the doorway, blocking it as he threw the door open. "You!" he shouted to a passing officer. "Take these two into custody. I want them held for questioning."

Chapter

13

THE POLICE OFFICER GAZED at the Hardys a little oddly as he led them away. Frank figured it wasn't every day people were arrested in the chief's office.

Lawrence's voice followed them down the hall. "Get me the Millerton police. . . ." He was already savoring the triumph of siccing the local law on the unsuspecting Chief Collig.

The desk officer was as surprised at this in-house arrest as Frank and Joe's guard. He had to interrupt Lawrence's call to Chief Gilmartin to get a charge.

"They're not being charged with anything," Lawrence said, emerging from his office. "They're just assisting us in investigating the Collig case." He gave the Hardys a sidelong glance.

"Assisting!" Joe burst out. "We tried to assist, by telling you not to go after Collig, but to go after Ray Bozeman. He's the one—" Joe's angry words were cut off as a heavy hand landed on his shoulder.

The man in the suit with the heavy hand was a stranger, but Frank figured out his job from the look on the other cops' faces. Another of Lawrence's Internal Affairs shoo-flies, he realized as the man started leading them away.

"Hold on a second!" Joe resisted the pull on his shoulder. "Don't we get a phone call?"

"There's no need for a phone call." The man's voice was snide. "That's only when people are charged with crimes. You're just answering some questions to aid our investigation."

"You can't keep us here like this! Either charge us or let us go!"

Frank grabbed his brother's arm. "I think Dad would want us to help the police." He stared deep into Joe's eyes. Remember Dad's license, that look said.

Joe shut up. "Okay, let's get the questions over with."

The shoo-fly led them to an interrogation room. He was tall and bland faced, with an expensive haircut and a designer suit. Another would-be smooth character, Frank thought. "I'm Detective Belknap, by the way," the investigator told them with a nasty smile. "Be back in a minute. Don't go away, now."

"All the comforts of home." Frank flopped down on the unyielding seat of a wooden chair and stared around the room. There wasn't much to see: a bare table, walls covered in sound-deadening acoustical tile. One wall was a huge, floor-to-ceiling mirror. "Here's another fine mess your big mouth has gotten us into," Frank added.

Joe felt bad. All too late he realized that Frank had never mentioned seeing Chief Collig. If he hadn't mentioned it, Lawrence wouldn't have had any reason to hold them. "Hey, Frank, I'm sorry—"

His brother raised a hand. "Don't say any more. You know how they set up interrogation rooms." He glanced up at the light fixture, sure there was a bug up there. Then he glanced at the probable two-way mirror, remembering the VCR in the acting chief's office. "Smile. Right now, we're probably on Parkervision."

"If you ask me, the acting chief is more into acting than being chief. He's not investigating the Collig case. He just wants to nail down his new job. And he doesn't want any inconvenient facts getting in his way."

Belknap came in, carrying a notepad. "Okay, let's get down to cases here. What time did you leave for Millerton?"

He continued to ask for every detail of the trip on the interstate. At first Frank thought it was some kind of strategy, a trick to trip them up.

Maybe the acting chief had some suspicions that they'd helped smuggle Collig out of town.

But Belknap didn't pounce on any discrepancies in their stories. He just slowly wrote down every word on his pad. Every time Frank or Joe tried to move ahead, he'd bring them back with some nitpicking detail.

"How many newspaper volumes were in the library?" he asked.

A little farther along, it was, "Was this Preznowski wearing a tie?"

Joe stared. "What difference does that make?" he asked. "If you're that interested, you could ask your own guys who were at his office."

"I want to get the complete story here." Belknap raised his eyes from his pad. "Don't be in such a hurry. We have lots of time."

Frank and Joe understood. This wasn't an interrogation—it was a farce. Lawrence had obviously ordered his flunky to waste as much time as possible. Meanwhile, the acting chief was moving heaven and earth to get Collig captured in Millerton. Maybe Lawrence thought they were in cahoots with Collig. In any case, he was making sure they couldn't get to a phone to warn Collig.

In a weird way, though, the boring questions set off Frank's mind to reexamine the events of their trip. "So this Potts guy looked at Collig and saw what he thought was a ghost?" Belknap said. "What were his exact words?"

" 'Young Collig—another ghost trying to kill me!' " Suddenly Frank sat bolt upright on his uncomfortable chair. "Of course! *Another* ghost!"

Joe and Belknap stared at him. "What are you talking about?" Joe asked.

"Potts looked at Collig—a guy from his past—and saw a ghost. But he'd seen *another* ghost that night—the guy who shot at him. And there's nobody left around here from those old days but—"

"Ray Bozeman!" Joe mouthed so Belknap wouldn't hear him. "We suspected it, but this would be solid evidence! If we can prove that he shot at Potts, then Lawrence will have to take your theory seriously," he finished up in a whisper. He turned, eager to plead their case with Belknap. Then his shoulders fell. "But we can't prove it. Potts is the only one who saw Bozeman shooting at him. And the last time we saw him, that old man was a complete basket case."

"Nobody who has actually *seen* Bozeman is in condition to talk about him," Frank mused. "Unless—"

He turned to Belknap. "What's the latest word on Commissioner DeCampo and Rod Vernon? Have either of them regained consciousness yet?"

Their questioner didn't mind side conversations that took up more time, but he shook his head. "They're still more dead than alive, and they're still in the intensive care unit. With luck they'll pull through. So Collig won't go up for a murder rap." Belknap smiled nastily. "Just attempted murder."

"Collig isn't the one who tried to kill those guys," Joe burst out. "It's his old police partner, Ray Bozeman. Bozeman took shots at us. He threw a bomb at us on the interstate."

"Hold on, hold on, now. You haven't mentioned anything about a bomb so far." Belknap checked the point on his pencil and prepared to start writing again.

"Do you have guards at the hospital?" Frank interrupted.

"I suppose so. Why?"

"Because those two unconscious men are the only ones who can name Bozeman as the one behind the accusations. He tried to kill us when we started getting close to his secret." Frank turned to Belknap, grim-faced. "What do you think he'd do to people who could *prove* it?"

Joe leaned toward the man. "The last time we saw him, Bozeman was driving a tan station wagon, maybe ten years old. At least tell Lawrence to keep a lookout for it. If he turns up near the hospital, those men are in danger."

"Yeah." Belknap started to rise from his chair. "I'd better tell—"

Then he froze in midmovement. The expression on his face was the kind that usually appeared on practical-joke victims.

"You really had me going there for a second."
The man plopped down in his seat. "Sure. Go
tell Lawrence to put out an all-points bulletin on
a guy who exists only in your imagination. That
would put me in real good with the chief."

"Acting chief," Frank corrected him.

Belknap gave him a dirty look. "He'll be chief
soon enough, after we put Collig away. And then
he'll need a captain to run the I.A. unit."

Before he could say any more, the door to
the interrogation room opened. Con Riley stood
framed in the doorway. "Hey, Belknap, the acting chief needs some backup. He's tracking
down a report that Collig has been seen near
Bayport General, and he wants all his best people patrolling the area. Take Krebs and a squad
car."

"Near the hospital, huh?" Belknap flashed the
boys a triumphant smile. Then he rushed out the
door, hefting the pistol holster under his arm.

Con waited until Belknap was well gone. Then
he suddenly acted as if he'd just noticed the
boys. "Why, Frank and Joe Hardy! What are
you doing here?" It wasn't very good acting,
Frank decided.

"Parker Lawrence is holding us for 'questioning,'" Joe said. "We've been trapped with
that idiot for more than an hour."

"Well, there's no one to question you now,"
Riley said. "I guess you can go."

Frank studied Con intently. "What's going on

here? You weren't around before. How did you know we were here?"

"As one of you suggested a little earlier, the walls here have ears—and eyes." Con nodded toward the wall-length mirror. "That thing is two-way. Anybody next door can see and hear everything going on in here."

He smiled. "And sometimes I do paperwork in that room, away from the hustle and bustle."

"Thanks, Con." Joe rose from his chair. "We're out of here."

"Now, boys." Con waved a finger at them. "I want you to go straight home. No going off with your friends for pizza or stopping by the hospital to see if there's any excitement there." He gave them a broad wink.

"You mean that Collig was actually spotted near Bayport General?" Frank asked.

"Yes, indeed. I wouldn't think of sending crack investigators like Belknap and Krebs on a wild-goose chase. We got a call from the owner of a candy store in that area. Chief Collig had stopped in to buy some Sen-sen. Funny thing about that," Con said. "The chief *hates* Sen-sen."

"You think it's a phony?" Joe said.

"No, the store owner knows Collig—he's sure he recognized him." Riley steered them out of the interrogation room and toward the front entrance. "Maybe the chief thinks like you—and made a brief personal appearance to draw a lot of cops to the streets around Bayport General. Maybe there's a good reason for them to be there."

They were outside now. Riley waved them off.

"Thanks, Con," Frank said. "We owe you."

The boys dashed down the front stairs and out to their van. "Next stop, Bayport General," Frank announced.

"Lawrence took that tip pretty seriously," Joe said, looking out the van window. "Half the force must be cruising these streets."

Joe wasn't looking for police cars, though. He was scanning the streets for a glimpse of a tan station wagon. "I guess there's one good thing about having a bomb thrown at you. You're sure to remember the car it came from."

The streets were crowded with parked cars of every description, but Joe saw no tan station wagons.

"Okay. What do you say we check the hospital parking lot— Frank! There it is!" Joe nearly went out the window, pointing at a car parked under a light in a corner of the lot. These were the least convenient parking spaces—the ones farthest from the hospital entrance. As a result, cars were pretty sparse.

Frank whipped the van into an empty spot on the street. "Anyone in the wagon?" he asked.

Joe peered over at the target vehicle. "Doesn't seem to be."

"I think we'd better get over there and check it out, fast." Frank opened his door and stepped from the van. "Any holes in the fence?"

Joe had always been a shortcut-spotter. In a moment he found where someone had cut a slit in the Cyclone fencing around the lot.

The Hardys slipped through and were halfway to the station wagon when Frank suddenly said, "Funny."

"What's funny?" Joe turned to look where Frank was staring.

"That little fenced-off area in that far corner—they always have a chain and padlock on the gate."

"What for?"

Frank gave his brother a look. "That's where they store the tanks of ether and oxygen. The hospital needs both gases for surgery, but keeps them on the far end of the property because they're too flammable. A spark could set off a terrible fire or explosion."

His eyes suddenly grew wide. "Oh, no."

Joe was already running for the open gate.

Inside the fence a waist-high brick wall surrounded the gas stockpile. The big metal canisters were taller than the boys.

"There's the lock and chain," Joe said. "One link snipped through."

"And here's something that sure doesn't belong." Frank pointed at a reddish brown bundle of waxy sticks, wired up and attached to

123

some kind of mechanism. It was jammed into the middle of the gas tanks.

"That dynamite plus the gas—if it went off, we'd probably need a new hospital." Frank whispered as if he were afraid to wake the bomb up.

"Good thing we found it," Joe said. "Bozeman must have planted it, then headed out of range."

"Almost, kid—except for one thing," a voice said from behind them.

Joe whirled around, then froze under the glare of a tall, pale man. It wasn't the glare that stopped him. It was the big, blue steel .38 revolver in the man's hand.

"I haven't left yet," Ray Bozeman said.

Chapter

14

"HELLO, MR. BOZEMAN." It took every bit of nerve Frank Hardy had to keep his voice steady as he faced Ezra Collig's old partner.

Maybe once, Frank thought, Ray Bozeman had had a handsome face. But age and a hard life had changed it. Bozeman's blond hair had receded and gone a dingy gray. His flesh had shriveled up until his face looked as tight as a fist—all nose and cheekbones. His skin was pasty white, as if he'd been living under a rock—or in prison.

The only thing alive in Bozeman's face were his faded blue eyes. They glittered with a mad intensity.

"Don't try anything stupid," Bozeman snapped as Frank and Joe took a step toward the gate to get out of the enclosure. "I was the best shot on the Millerton force. Did Collig ever tell you that? *I said don't move!*"

Bozeman kicked the gate shut. "Back up till you've got that brick wall behind you. Good. Now sit on the ground. I want your legs straight out and your hands under your butts. *Move!*"

Frank realized they had no choice. The gun was scary enough, but Bozeman's eyes left no doubt of what he'd do if they tried anything.

Frank and Joe took the position that Bozeman ordered them into. They knew that without the use of their legs or hands, there was no way they could move quickly. They were helpless, a hundred feet from the hospital, shut into a little-used corner of the parking lot.

Bozeman allowed himself a brief, wolfish grin. Stained dentures flashed at them—the cheap kind made for prison inmates. "Smart boys," Bozeman said. "I don't know what a bullet in those gas tanks would do, but it's better not to find out, eh?"

Now his eyes glowed with evil triumph. "After all, we've got to save them for the *big* bang. I don't think it will be as powerful as you said, but it should be enough to take out Vernon and DeCampo—and at least half the hospital."

He smiled again, showing his cheap teeth. "It will also blow away Ezra Collig's last hope for clearing himself."

Bozeman flashed the butt of the gun at them

for an instant. There was a big gold stamp on it, with the seal of the Bayport Police. "I stopped off at Collig's house earlier and picked this up. Good and recognizable. It was one of the awards he got as a national top cop. I'll leave it someplace where it can be found after the explosion. Even that empty uniform of an acting chief should be able to handle things from there."

"Do you actually know Parker Lawrence?" Frank said. "We wondered about that."

"I know *about* him, the big jerk." Bozeman gave them another wolfish grin. "But he doesn't know about me. Soon no one will."

"What about Len Potts?" Joe spoke up desperately. "He recognized you in the alley, you know."

"Big deal," Bozeman sneered. "I know what the sound of shots does to him. If they get him back together again—and that's a big if—he may not even remember. By then Collig will already be in the joint. And who's going to listen to some crazy man? No," he finished proudly, "I planned it right. Collig will rot in jail, just like I did."

Bozeman's fish-belly face was the picture of successful revenge. "I had a long time to think while I was in the joint—about mistakes I made, chances I missed, people I blamed. I realized finally there was only one person responsible for all the trouble in my life—that blasted Collig."

His face twitched with hate. "If that stupid

kid had only kept his mouth shut, I woulda made sergeant, back there in Millerton. Sergeant, with a sweet racket—"

Frank blinked. From the tone of Bozeman's voice, it sounded as if he were describing paradise.

"And I didn't have to stop with sergeant, you know. A go-getter could get promoted in those days, even if he didn't have some fancy college-boy degree."

"Chief Bozeman?" Joe scoffed.

"Nah. But Lieutenant Bozeman, maybe captain. That's all I would have needed. I'd have been running that town." For a second his face softened with thoughts of what might have been. Then his features tightened up. "But no. A dumb rookie just off the turnip truck had to play saint, open his mouth, and ruin everything."

"Collig really didn't know about your scam with the Policemen's Fund," Frank said. "He really thought it was a charity."

Bozeman grinned mockingly. "I needed an honest man to make the collections. When any of my pals took the bag around, they always skimmed off the top." His face went cold. "If I'd thought Collig would rat on me, I'd have shot him like a dog thirty-five years ago."

"Some cop you were," Joe muttered.

"I was a good cop!" Bozeman snarled. "Smart enough to catch a lot of crooks—and catch myself some extra change. I had a sweet racket set up until Collig finked. Then I couldn't keep jobs long enough. Sooner or later it came out. 'Weren't you the guy in Millerton . . . ?' They watched me like a hawk. Every time I got a little action started, I was out. Then I couldn't even *get* a job. So I started working the other side of the street."

"Until that bank job put you away," Joe said.

Bozeman nodded. "I was coming up for parole when I read this article in a magazine about the national top cop awards. And who do I see but Ezra Collig, Chief of Bayport P.D."

Frank and Joe exchanged glances. It was just as they'd thought. "So then you started checking out your old partner," Frank said.

"I still had time on my hands and the prison library." Bozeman leaned forward. "So I read all about Bayport and Collig—like the big scandal when the town supervisor got killed."

He chuckled. "Old Ezra sure muffed that case, didn't he?" Then his face went cold again. "Now that I think about it, you were in on that, too. Frank and Joe Hardy. I should have known to watch out for you."

"Collig came through that case pretty well," Joe said. "He arrested the bad guys and kept his job."

"Yeah, Honest Ezra, the only one to keep his job from the old administration. But I know politicians, and I figured someone would have the knives out for the chief."

"Mark DeCampo," Frank said.

"I could always figure the angles," Bozeman said. "DeCampo was hot to find corruption. He even brought in his own stooge, Lawrence, to probe for it. Then I saw this new guy on the local news—Rod Vernon, a great investigative reporter in his own mind. He got bounced from the network and needed a story to get back."

"So you gave it to him," Joe said.

Bozeman smirked. "I thought Vernon was going to bust a blood vessel when I started leaking stuff to him. He took the ball and ran with it."

"Vernon was a lousy journalist," Frank said flatly. "He never bothered to double-check anything you passed on to him."

"Which made him perfect for my purposes," Bozeman said. "Besides, how could he check my story? It happened so long ago, many of the people involved are dead or have moved away. Collig had this one little chink in the armor of his reputation, and I managed to fill it full of dirt."

Bozeman smiled so widely, Frank almost expected his false teeth to pop out.

"I figured a nice quiet whispering campaign would be enough to ruin Collig, but Vernon wanted to turn it into a circus, and so did DeCampo. He wanted hearings, an investigation, the whole nine yards. They were too clumsy in nailing Collig, so people began feeling sorry for him—the big drip!" He frowned. "I could see the handwriting on the wall when that editorial came out, asking for solid proof."

"DeCampo and Vernon wanted you to step forward." The picture was shaping up just as Frank had suspected. "And you didn't dare do that."

"They expected me on that dock with all sorts of goods on Collig. DeCampo was planning a major news conference to unveil me or something. Vernon, of course, would have a front-row seat. But I had a better idea, one that would really nail old Ezra. I blew up the dock and the two guys howling loudest for his blood."

"You figured that Collig would be the prime suspect," Frank said.

"And that Parker Lawrence would railroad him right to prison," Joe added.

"All it took was a midnight visit to a local construction site for some dynamite. Vernon played into my hands, telling me about that rental car he was going to use." Bozeman tried to act modest. "I always had a way with auto locks."

"But it didn't work as you planned," Joe pointed out. "Vernon and DeCampo didn't die, and Collig didn't let himself get arrested."

"And you two came sticking your noses in." Bozeman gave them a cold glare. "You turned up at the dock—following Vernon, I guess."

Frank and Joe nodded. "Then we found the

THE HARDY BOYS CASEFILES

chief's car, and we were broadcast saying that we were going to Millerton,'' Frank said. "You must have heard it on the morning news and followed us."

Their captor looked hard at Frank. "You called me Bozeman, so I guess you found out everything. Right?"

"Enough," Joe said. "The only problem is, we don't have enough proof."

Bozeman gave them a savage grin. "Good. That was the only thing that worried me when I tried to blow you up. But after this blast, my troubles will be over."

Behind them, they heard a rattle from the Cyclone fencing.

"Bozeman!" a voice yelled raggedly.

Frank stared as Chief Collig stalked toward them. He had bags under his eyes, and his clothes were soiled and rumpled.

But the gun in his hand looked all business— and it was pointed at Ray Bozeman.

Chapter

15

THIS IS LIKE the final gunfight scene in an old western flick, Joe thought.

He and Frank were the helpless audience, just like the townspeople in those ancient cowboy movies. The question was, would the guy in the white hat win this time?

The two men squared off, guns in hand. They made a strange contrast after thirty-five years. Back then Collig had been a raw-boned, skinny kid; Bozeman, tough, a leader. Now Collig had grown, and Bozeman had shrunk. His pale, gaunt face was like a skull as he stood glaring at the chief.

"How's it going, Ez?" Bozeman's voice was soft and silky.

Collig's eyes widened at the use of his old nickname.

"You know," Bozeman went on, "I was telling these kids how I was the best shot in the old Millerton days. You were always so bad, Ez. I bet I could still aim, plug you, and blow away the kids before you could shoot me."

He smiled. "That is, if I wanted to play fair."

Bozeman whipped around, his gun aimed straight at Frank's head. "Drop the gun, Collig, or I put a bullet in the smart boy's brain. You know I mean it." The ex-con's voice was flat and deadly. "Even if you shoot me, you lose him."

Silence seemed to stretch for an eternity. Then came a clatter as Collig let his gun fall to the pavement.

Ray Bozeman turned so he could keep one eye on the Hardys, the other on Collig. "Kick the gun over here, Ez."

Collig bristled. "Don't call me Ez. That's what my friends used to call me, and you were never my friend."

Bozeman's face grew even more pinched. "You're in no position to give orders," he said, raising his gun. "I can call you anything I like. If you don't kick that thing over, I'll call you dead."

Face frozen, Collig kicked his revolver over. He tensed as Bozeman stood over it.

His old partner chuckled, a chilling sound.

"Gonna rush me when I bend to pick it up? Dream on, rookie." He gestured with the gun again. "On the ground, belly down, hands behind your head. *Now!*"

It took a moment for Collig to assume that humiliating position. Frank and Joe could only watch, sitting on their hands. Only when the chief was completely helpless did Bozeman stoop for the other gun.

"They can call me Two-Gun Bozeman," he said, slipping Collig's piece into his pocket. He kept the chief's .38 revolver aimed at Collig's head.

Bozeman walked over to the prone police chief. Suddenly he whirled around, his gun covering Joe. "No moving," he said, waggling a finger. "Someone could get hurt." His gun shifted to aim at Collig's head. "Do you want the chief to go before his time?"

Joe sagged back, giving up his attempt to surge to his feet. There was no way to rise quickly from his stupid position.

Keeping his gun behind Collig's ear, Bozeman began to frisk the chief.

"And what do we have here?" he asked, searching a rear pocket. Bozeman began to laugh. "Good old Ez, a cop to the end," he said, drawing out a pair of handcuffs.

"Well, I may just have a use for these." The ex-con snapped one of the bracelets onto Collig's right wrist. "Now up." He stepped back as the chief ponderously struggled to his feet. "Walk over to that gate." Bozeman stayed out of reach, his gun trained on Collig's head.

When Collig reached the gate, Bozeman stopped him at the fence beside it. "Assume the position," he ordered.

The chief leaned his hands against the Cyclone fence, in the traditional position of a captured felon. The empty handcuff bracelet rattled against the metal fence.

"Come on, how long have you been a cop? You know better than that!" Bozeman's foot hooked Collig's shins, forcing his feet back. The crook's free hand shoved into the small of the chief's back. Collig was forced off balance, forced to hold his weight on his hands, helpless again.

Bozeman smiled and clicked the free handcuff bracelet around the gatepost and gate. The entrance to the gas storage area was locked again, trapping the boys inside, with Ezra Collig chained to the fence.

"To show you what a nice guy I am, I'll let your last moments be comfortable. See those bottles of dangerous gas in there, Ez? That's a bomb. It'll blow you, DeCampo, Vernon, and these kids to kingdom come. But till it goes off, I'll let you stand up."

Collig staggered back to his feet. Joe and Frank rose, too, stretching cramped muscles.

Bozeman still played his parody of a concerned host. "Glad to see you could make it, Ez. How'd you get here?" He pointed his gun to make it clear he wanted an answer.

"I hitched on a truck," Collig answered gruffly. "It was easy sneaking back to Bayport. I got out of Millerton before they sealed the place up, and the roadblocks here stopped only cars heading out."

"Well, I can't say how happy I am that you're here." Bozeman's voice suddenly turned cold and ominous. "Because I want to see your face when I talk to you, you miserable—"

Thirty years of hatred poured out in a torrent of abuse. Again the Hardys heard Bozeman's complaint, in fouler words because the supposed cause of Bozeman's misfortune was there to hear it.

"If you're a cop today, it's because I *made* you one!" Bozeman screamed. "You owed me, and how did you pay me back? You ratted on me!"

"You used me!" Collig shouted back. "You were my partner, and partners are supposed to look out for each other. Instead, you turned me into the bagman for your cheap little racket!"

"What? You were annoyed because I didn't tell you what the scam was? I was thinking of letting you in on it—"

"If you had," Collig cut him off, "I'd have turned you in sooner."

Bozeman looked like a complete maniac as he

raised his gun. Frank was sure he was going to blow the chief away.

With an effort, though, Bozeman brought his arm down. "No. That was what I wanted at first. I wanted to kill you," he said in a hoarse voice. "Then I thought how much better it would be if I ruined your life first. I wanted to rip away your honor, drag your pride through the mud. Everything you built up, I wanted to dirty. And you see how easy it was?"

Bozeman's laugh didn't sound quite human. It was more the howl of a triumphant beast. "Your reputation? Vernon was happy to smear that with just the barest suggestion of a story. Your career? DeCampo and Lawrence couldn't wait to break that in little pieces. And after tonight—well, see this?"

Out of reach Bozeman showed the chief the butt of the gun he'd stolen from Collig's house. A cruel smile twisted his lips as he watched as Collig recognized it. "I thought it only fitting. You got this as a national award for being a top cop. That's how I found out where you've been all these years. After this bomb goes off, there won't be enough of you around to identify. But if I leave this, it's sure to implicate you in the blast."

He laughed. "After tonight, anytime anyone mentions your name, there'll only be disgusted silence."

Collig hung his head.

Bozeman loved it. "The only thing I regret is that your old lady croaked before I got things rolling. That would have been perfect." He started talking in a high-pitched voice. " 'Oh, Ezra, these awful things can't be true, can they?' " He gave a brutal guffaw. "And if that didn't kill her, I'd have done the job myself—a hit-and-run, maybe."

Frank caught the flash in Collig's eye as he heard that. It wasn't the look of a man in pain. Why is he staring at the ground, then? Frank wondered. What's he thinking of?

He realized then that Collig wasn't gazing at the ground, he was staring fixedly at Frank's feet. Frank glanced down. No, it wasn't his feet. There was a small metal ring on the ground, with a tiny key. The chief had managed to toss the key to his handcuffs next to Frank!

Frank dropped to the ground, doing his best to act as if he'd given up all hope.

"You—up!" Bozeman shouted, whirling on Frank. "Stand up and take it like a man."

While I take it from a maniac, Frank thought as he pushed himself up. While his hand was on the ground, he palmed the key. Then, on his feet, he faced Bozeman while flashing the key behind his back to Joe.

Frank held out the key, the movement hidden by his body. Joe immediately grabbed their ticket to freedom. "On my signal," Frank whispered.

It was probably a hopeless fight, but they had to try. If Joe could unlock the chief's handcuff from the gate, he and the chief might be able to overpower Bozeman. Frank would have to disable the bomb. Bozeman might shoot them all, but they might just save the hospital. Any gunfire would draw the cops prowling the immediate area.

"You won't get away with this, Bozeman," Collig said. "I knew you were behind everything since I headed for Millerton. Finally that stupid picture came back to me—the two of us and the moose head at Minty's. I realized you must have been working with Vernon and DeCampo and that you had to finish them off. They needed protection. I couldn't order it, but I could draw it here."

"How?" Bozeman sneered.

"Easy. I walked into a store where the owner knew me and bought some candy. This area is now crawling with cops."

"Even so, they're looking for you, not me," Bozeman said. "But thanks for the tip, old buddy. I'd better get started. There's a radio detonator in my car. I'll take it a safe distance, hit the button, and watch the fireworks."

He stepped away from the enclosure, then turned back. "I'll be safe, but I'll still be able to see you. Don't try anything, because I can still shoot and hit you. And remember—"

"Yeah, right," Joe said. "You were the best shot on the Millerton force."

Bozeman brought his gun up. "You know, kid, if I had more time, I'd teach you some manners. But it would be a waste, what with your short life expectancy."

He turned and was halfway to his car when Frank whispered, "Now!"

Joe grabbed the handcuff bracelet locking the gate, jammed in the key, and twisted it.

Frank leapt for the bomb amid the gas cylinders. Whatever happened, he had to disarm it!

Ezra Collig tore the handcuff loose and flung open the gate. The moment it was open, Joe charged out. It was probably hopeless, but he was going to try to tackle Bozeman.

The chief's old partner whirled around at the noise. He was aiming the chief's revolver in his left hand before Joe had taken two steps. Joe hurled himself forward anyway.

With his right hand, Bozeman whipped out the gun he'd just taken from Collig.

Collig was moving his right hand, too. It slid to his waistband. As Joe raced past, he saw the little automatic appear in the chief's fingers.

Then, at the same time, the three guns exploded.

Chapter
16

JOE KNEW WHERE one of Bozeman's bullets went. It whistled just past his right ear.

He had no idea where Bozeman's other bullet flew.

But he knew where Ezra Collig's shot went.

Ray Bozeman twisted and fell as if he'd been kicked. The big, blue steel revolver flew from his suddenly nerveless fingers, but the gun in his right hand came up for another try at the chief.

Collig, trained police officer that he was, cried, "Freeze, Bozeman!"

Ray Bozeman just smiled. He didn't have to play by police rules.

Joe kept charging. Bozeman wavered for a second, choosing his target—Collig or Joe. To Joe's eyes, the muzzle of the gun appeared large enough to fire cannonballs.

Okay, he told himself. When in doubt, punt.

Still on the run, he launched a kick at Bozeman's gun hand. His foot caught the gun and tore it from the ex-con's grasp, sending it arcing fifteen feet away.

"Three points for our side!" Joe crowed.

Chief Collig came trotting over, his little automatic at the ready. Shaking his head at Joe, he said, "That was the bravest stunt I ever saw anyone try."

Joe grinned.

"It was also the stupidest. What if he'd shot you?"

"Um," Joe said.

"You've got guts, but it wouldn't hurt to use your brains once in a while." Collig turned to keep Bozeman covered.

Joe stared in fascination at the tiny gun, scarcely larger than the chief's palm. "What *is* that?" he asked.

"A backup pistol," Collig replied. "Also known as a belly gun because it's small enough to fit inside the waist of your pants." He kicked the big blue revolver farther away from Bozeman. His ex-partner glared helplessly up at him.

"You always were lousy at patting people down, Ray," Collig said. "And I've gotten to be a better shot over the years."

Then he turned to Joe. "How's your first aid,

young man? I believe this gent has a bullet in his shoulder.''

Frank joined them. "The bomb is dead," he announced. "But not Mr. Bozeman, I'm glad to see."

"No, I think he'll be back among his friends in the state pen pretty soon," Joe said, using Bozeman's shirt to stanch his wound. "After all, we heard him admit that the chief was innocent in that extortion scam."

"Your word against mine," Bozeman gasped.

"And your fingerprints on the bomb," Frank pointed out. "I think that will help make a case."

Bayport P.D. squad cars came screaming from all four directions into the parking lot.

"Somebody should tell Lawrence not to run the sirens by the hospital," Collig said. "This is supposed to be a quiet zone."

The cars pulled into a semicircle, pinning them in a wall of headlights. Doors flew open and officers braced behind them, aiming their guns two-handed. Parker Lawrence's voice came over a bullhorn: "Collig! Put down the gun! We have you surrounded!"

"Okay, Lawrence." Collig tossed the gun to the side and raised his hands. "We've got a wounded man here." He nodded toward the hospital. "Maybe you should get him some medical attention."

As soon as the gun was down, several men

approached the chief. In fact, the area was swarming with police units and officers, all drawn from the surrounding blocks by the sound of shots.

"Another attempted murder charge," Detective Belknap said importantly, reaching out to grab Collig's shoulder. "You have the right to remain silent, Collig."

"It was self-defense," Joe said.

"That's what they all say." Then Belknap recognized him. "What are *you* doing here?"

"Just what I was about to ask." Parker Lawrence advanced on them grimly. He looked very impressive, a police warm-up jacket over his bullet-proof vest—all ready for any camera crews.

"I warned you what would happen if you kept interfering in this case." Lawrence poked a finger into Frank's chest. "You could be considered accessories to this crime. So answer the officer. What where you doing here?"

"Stopping a second murder attempt on DeCampo and Vernon," Frank answered crisply. "This is the man who made both tries." He pointed at Bozeman, who was still groaning. "In there you'll see the bomb he planted." Frank pointed to the gas tank storage enclosure.

"Bomb?" Lawrence repeated.

Frank sighed. "It's been deactivated."

"His name is Ray Bozeman, by the way," Joe added. "He started the smear campaign that

THE HARDY BOYS CASEFILES

DeCampo, Vernon, and—'' He smiled at Lawrence. ''Well, I guess you know who else was involved in that.''

Parker Lawrence was standing with his mouth open as the news van arrived from WBPT. Obviously, Frank thought, things were moving too fast for him.

Grinning, Chief Collig turned around and put his hands behind him. He jingled the handcuffs that still hung from one wrist. ''Well, come on, acting chief. Clap these on and take me to headquarters. You can get the keys from Joe Hardy, there.''

He glanced at Lawrence over his shoulder. ''And by the way,'' he added, ''I wouldn't get too attached to the job of acting chief, if I were you.''

Two days later the boys sat in their living room over a copy of the *Bayport Times*. The banner headline read ''Out of the Bag.'' A big photo showed a grinning Chief Collig holding out his handcuffs—and the key to them.

''So, Bozeman finally cracked,'' Joe said, reading the article.

''He didn't have much choice,'' Frank pointed out. ''The evidence was piled up against him. It wasn't just his fingerprints on the bomb. The truth about his old extortion scam started to surface.''

''How?'' Joe started to read faster.

"It's on page four. Using the list of phone numbers for Millerton police retirees, the *Times* finally found somebody who knew the inside story about Collig's turning Bozeman in. It was some guy living in Arizona. He was a pal of the police captain there—Frazee—who'd told him the whole thing."

Frank grinned. "Needless to say, the Internal Affairs Unit is very embarrassed."

"Sounds like they may need a new boss," Joe said.

"There is talk of Captain Parker Lawrence going back wherever he came from," Frank agreed. "By the way, did you read the sidebar about Rod Vernon? He's conscious, and he's admitted that Bozeman was his primary source on the corruption story."

"Another straw that broke Bozeman's back," Joe guessed.

"It may also do a job on DeCampo," Frank said. "Vernon had to admit why he was meeting DeCampo on the dock. So the whole story of their secret association is out now. There are a lot of red faces at City Hall. The first thing they did was give Collig his job back."

"Sounds like DeCampo may come out of his coma to find he's in political limbo," Joe said. "Couldn't happen to a nicer guy."

He flopped back on the couch. "Well, thanks, Frank. Guess I won't have to read all this now."

Frank was opening his mouth to reply when the phone rang. Frank picked it up.

"It's Con Riley," he told Joe, putting a hand over the receiver. "So, Con," he said, "what can we poor amateurs do for you?"

Frank's grin suddenly changed. "Really?" he said. "We'd completely forgotten about that. Just found them on the desk, huh?"

He listened a bit more. "We can? Great! No, we're leaving right away!"

Frank hung up and turned to Joe. "Come on. We have unfinished business at police headquarters."

"Unfinished?" Joe repeated.

"Dad's papers finally turned up from wherever Parker Lawrence had hidden them. You do want Dad to keep his P.I. license, don't you?"

The atmosphere at police headquarters was very different from that of their last visit. The only nervous officers were the ones from the Internal Affairs Unit. Frank watched their interrogator, Belknap, scurrying around in the background. Instead of wearing a suit, he was back in uniform and carrying a big stack of files.

Con Riley gave the Hardys a cheerful greeting from the booking desk. "Go right in, gentlemen. Straight down the hall—I think you know the way."

The pebbled glass door with the word *Chief*

in gold letters was half open. "Come in," Chief Collig invited.

He was seated behind the same old wooden desk with new piles of paper. Parker Lawrence's TV and VCR were gone, but Frank noticed that the computer remained.

"I'm going to take a stab at learning to use that thing," Collig said, following Frank's eyes. "Have to keep up with the times, you know."

A good night's sleep had erased the dark rings from under his eyes. In fact, Joe couldn't remember seeing the chief look better. It was as if ten years had rolled off him.

Chief Collig held up a familiar-looking manila envelope. "Here are your father's papers, signed and sealed," he said. "I've already spoken with the people in the licensing authority to explain why they'll be late."

"Thanks, Chief," Frank and Joe said.

"It was the least I could do to thank you two." Collig put his palms on the desk and stared up at the boys. "And I do want to thank you. Without your help, I'd probably still be hiding under a bush somewhere."

"I'm sure things would have worked out," Frank said.

"At some point," Collig said. "But thanks to you, the nightmare is over *now*. I really appreciate how you stood by me in spite of any past differences we might have had." The chief grinned. "And in spite of some rough moments along the way."

He stood up. "This was an odd case, taking me back to when I was young. It sort of reminded me of what it was like to be your age."

"It was pretty weird for us, too," Joe admitted.

"Yes, like a trip back in time, seeing what policing was like years back," Frank said. "I don't think I'll ever dismiss the old days as being simpler, though."

He met Collig's eyes. "It must have taken a whole lot of courage to break through the blue wall of silence."

The chief lowered his eyes for a second, saying nothing. Then he handed over Fenton Hardy's papers.

"Thanks again, men," he said, shaking hands with Frank and Joe. "I guess, in a way, we know one another a little better now."

"I guess so," Joe said.

Collig sat down again.

"Well, goodbye, Chief." Envelope tucked under his arm, Frank headed for the door.

"Hey, Hardys," Collig called after them as they stepped into the hallway. "Just remember. This won't cut any ice if you come horning in on one of my cases tomorrow."

Frank and Joe laughed.

"Okay," Joe said. "It'll be enemies as usual—the next time."

Frank and Joe's next case:

Frank and Joe are working security at the World Snowboarding Championships in Austria, and they're learning fast that the Alps can be as dangerous as they are beautiful—the perfect setting for sabotage. Ken Gibson is the number-one competitor and the number-one target. Reason: He's been leading a secret life!

The race is on, and the stakes are as steep as they get. Frank and Joe discover that both the Network and an underworld gang have gotten into the game. The Hardys are standing on top of a mountain of trouble—and it's about to explode under their feet . . . in *Height of Danger,* Case #56 in The Hardy Boys Casefiles™.

OKLAHOMA PUBLIC LIBRARY